CARING FOR HIS BABIES

BY

LILIAN DARCY

MILLS & BOON®

First published in Great Britain 2004
Harlequin Mills & Boon Limited,
Eton House, 18-24 Paradise Road, Richmond, Surrey TW9 1SR

Set in Times Roman 10½ on 12 pt.
07-0904-48125

Printed and bound in Great Britain
by Antony Rowe Ltd, Chippenham, Wiltshire

CHAPTER ONE

THE phone line between Sydney and Riyadh was far clearer than Keelan had expected it to be, and there weren't the few seconds of delay he sometimes experienced with international calls. He'd had more difficult connections when talking to his cousin two suburbs away.

'Tell me about the babies,' said Jessica Russell, at the other end of the line.

It was four o'clock in the afternoon in Riyadh, but her voice sounded slightly husky as if she'd only just woken. Maybe she was working nights and sleeping days. Whatever her hours, she would be on a plane two days from now, heading home to Australia to meet her tiny new patients and Keelan himself.

'Well, Tavie's a lot better off than Tam at this stage...' Keelan began inadequately.

Keeping the cordless phone against his ear, he paced to the window of his study and looked out into the night. The harbour-scape appeared the same as always—a wide stripe of glittering black water, dancing with blue and red neon reflected from the city on the opposite shore and framed by a huge Moreton Bay fig tree on the right and his neighbour's house on the left.

So much else had changed, however, in just ten days.

'That's why I...we...need you on board so soon,' he continued.

Why had he changed the pronoun to 'we'? he had time to wonder, as he paused for breath. His various cousins, uncles and aunts applauded what he was doing, but had all declared, not without cause, that they had too much going on in their own lives to get involved on a practical level.

His mother had shown more enthusiasm and desire to help. She'd visited the hospital on the weekend, but she lived almost four hours away, north of Newcastle, and technically she was no relation at all to the twins. He wasn't going to foist on her the grandchildren of the woman who'd broken up her marriage twenty-three years ago.

Dad should have stepped forward perhaps, but he seemed frankly terrified—quite paralysed—and ready to run a mile from any involvement. Was it grief, or regret, or the fact that the babies were so fragile and small?

'All going well,' Keelan finished, dragging his focus back to more practical concerns. 'The girl—Tavie—should be discharged next week.'

In a more perfect world the little girl twin would have been discharged into her mother's care, but Brooke—Keelan's half-sister—was dead and…

He revised his thought.

In a more perfect world, twenty-two-year-old Brooke would never have become pregnant in the first place, through one of her many unsuitable affairs, and even if she had, she would have sought the right prenatal care, the twins might not have been born so prematurely and Brooke would certainly have realised that the post-partum bleeding she'd experienced after her discharge from the hospital had been way heavier than it should have been.

Too many ifs.

Too much drama, in too short a time.

The babies were ten days old, having been born at just

over twenty-eight weeks gestation, and the little boy, Tam, was clinging to life by a thread. Brooke had collapsed in a café a week ago, but emergency treatment had come too late and she'd bled out in the ambulance on the way to the same hospital, North Sydney, where she'd given birth. The Hunter clan had survived the funeral—and the publicity—with its usual dignity and repressed emotion.

Keelan's ex-stepmother, Louise—Brooke's mother—had fallen apart in private afterwards, however. She was still heavily medicated, apparently, back home in Melbourne with her new husband, Phillip.

He'd told Keelan categorically, 'We can't take them. It just wouldn't work. Especially if they turn out to be delicate or damaged. I'm too old, and Louise isn't very strong emotionally. Especially now, of course. Some other arrangement will have to be made.'

Keelan had known, at that moment, that there was really only one option. Discounting the babies' father, since he'd disappeared from Brooke's life months ago, and they didn't even know his last name, Keelan was the babies' closest blood relative of an appropriate age for fatherhood. He was a paediatrician at North Sydney Hospital, and knew exactly the kinds of problems that the babies might face now and in the future.

So he'd adopt them himself.

It wouldn't be an ideal solution but, as he'd just concluded, this wasn't a perfect world. He felt uncomfortable about how much the babies' new nurse needed to know about all of this. With four generations of highly successful Hunter lawyers, doctors, politicians and financiers preceding him, Keelan valued privacy and discretion. He wondered uneasily just which boundaries he'd be able to keep in place during the coming months.

'So I'll mainly be settling in until that happens?' Jessica Russell asked over the phone. 'Until she's ready to come home?'

'Spending as much time with both of them at the hospital, I would hope,' he answered firmly. 'I'll be pushing for the earliest discharge that's safely possible, given your experience with preemies, so I'll want you liaising closely with the nurses in the unit and getting familiar with each baby's condition and needs. Settling in can happen in your own time.'

She gave a wry laugh. 'Is there going to be much of that? My own time, I mean. The twins themselves will call the shots on my hours.'

This comment reassured Keelan, yet served to confirm that he hadn't quite trusted her before, and probably still didn't. Wouldn't for a while, if he had any sense. This would be merely a job for her. She could never have the same investment in the twins' well-being as he did.

He'd intended to go through an agency here in Sydney, get someone local. He liked to make his own judgements about people. But a medical colleague in Adelaide had recommended Ms Russell, and when he had gone to a Sydney nursing agency, her name, by coincidence, had come up again.

'She registered with us quite recently, and has first-class credentials and references. I'd jump at her, if I were you. I imagine she'll be looking for a permanent hospital position before too long.'

Jessica had been working in a high-level neonatal unit in Saudi Arabia, but she'd had enough of it after two years and was about to come home. She would be ready to start exactly when Keelan wanted her—that was, immediately.

Keelan was wary of the coincidence rather than reassured by it. He didn't go in for 'signs'. But he couldn't ignore Ms Russell's level of experience when it was coupled with a recommendation from someone he trusted.

'Why's she been in Saudi, though?' he'd asked his colleague, Lukas Cheah, phoning the man for a second time in search of more details. 'It can be a dangerous part of the world for Westerners.'

'Not sure. A bit of a wanderer?'

'A risk-taker?'

'Not necessarily. Saving for a mortgage? Some nurses manage to build a nice bank balance over there. From what my wife has said—' Jane Cheah was also an NICU nurse, Keelan knew '—I don't think she has much family to fall back on.'

Keelan, in contrast, had far too much family. He felt the pressure sometimes. At other times he felt pride.

'Sounds as if you're not worried about working long, erratic hours,' he said to Ms Russell.

'Well, no, since it's obviously a requirement and, I assume, the reason for the…uh…generous salary you've offered. Anyway,' she added quickly, 'I've done it before.'

She sounded uncomfortable about discussing money. Keelan was, too. Probably for different reasons. The Hunter family had a fair bit of it, but he liked to be as discreet about that fact as possible. He went back to the subject of the twins' health and medical status instead.

'Let me give you more details about what you'll be dealing with. They were born somewhere between twenty-eight and twenty-nine weeks. The girl—Tavie—is significantly heavier and stronger.'

'What was her birth weight?'

'She was 1220 grams. Tam was just under a kilo—

990 grams—but we'll get to him later. I'll try and go through this systematically. Tavie is still on oxygen.'

'CPAP?'

'She started on a respirator, but yes, she's up to CPAP now.'

Of course Ms Russell knew the abbreviation—continuous positive airway pressure, delivering oxygen via a tube taped to the baby's face. It was good not to have to explain.

'She's also on light therapy for jaundice as of two days ago,' he continued. 'She had a heart murmur indicative of PDA—' again, it reassured him to use the abbreviation for the common preemie heart problem, patent ductus arteriosus, knowing she'd understand it '—but that's resolved on it's own, fortunately.'

'Sometimes those can re-open.'

'It'll be monitored, of course.'

'Gut problems? As and Bs?'

'Her gut is good, but she's still having recurrent apnoea and bradycardia episodes, yes. With you on board, she can be discharged with oxygen and monitors, if that's still necessary, and I expect it will be.'

'Yes.'

'We want to see her get back up to her birth weight and show some steady gain before her discharge in any case.'

'She's on tube feeds?'

'Yes.'

'And the boy—Tam—isn't so good, you said?'

He couldn't hold back a sigh. 'No, unfortunately. His heart problems are more serious. We…uh…realistically…don't know if he'll make it.'

'Sometimes they don't.' It wasn't an unsympathetic

line. She'd just seen it before, that was all, and knew there wasn't a lot to say.

'We heard a heart murmur when he was a couple of days old,' he continued, keeping to facts, not feelings. 'An echocardiogram showed two ventricular septal defects—VSDs.' It was one of the most common congenital heart defects, more prevalent in boys and more prevalent in twins than single births.

'Serious ones? Can they tell?'

'We're still hoping they may close over on their own, but so far they haven't. Four days ago his oxygen levels began dropping. They did another scan and found a third VSD, large, around 7 millimetres. He also showed coarctation of the aorta.'

'He wouldn't be strong enough for surgery yet,' she guessed. 'Although that thinned aorta must be a concern for you.'

'Definitely, but yes, before surgery we need to grow him and stabilise him, steer him past a few other risks.'

'Infection, gut problems, jaundice,' she murmured. 'Is he on bili lights, like his sister?'

'Yes.'

'I love bili lights—something we can do for them that doesn't cause them pain.'

'I know what you mean.'

'And they've lost their mother, too… Rough way to come into this world.' The husky note in her voice had deepened. 'I hope someone's told you what a heroic thing you're doing, Dr Hunter, taking them on.'

'There was no choice,' he answered shortly, wondering if he should have saved the story on their circumstances until he'd met the twins' nurse face to face.

She'd rubbed him up the wrong way with her statement, well intentioned though it had clearly been. He didn't want editorial commentary from an employee. A compliment like the one she'd just given him implied that she had the right to criticise as well, and she didn't. She was just a paid carer, chosen for her expertise not for her opinions and feelings.

Except…

Premature babies needed love. It was a medically established fact that fragile infants did better when they had periods of warm, peaceful body contact. Tavie and Tam needed Jessica Russell to care about them.

Keelan wasn't married or seriously involved with any woman right now. There was no other female under his roof to fill a maternal role, and yet he didn't want Ms Russell to get too close, or too indispensable, because eventually, inevitably, she would leave. What would that do to the babies, a few months down the track, if they'd become deeply attached to her?

Lord, this wasn't going to be easy!

Jessie put down the phone after Keelan Hunter's call and squinted out into the glare of the desert's afternoon light. Her eyes ached for the relief of Sydney's lush, almost tropical foliage. Two more days. It would be fun to try a new city, a place she'd only ever seen during a couple of brief holidays. And it might be refreshing to get back to some private nursing for a while, she told herself.

A feeling of restlessness tugged at her heart, dragging her spirits down. She'd been so *good*, so sensible these past two years. She'd lived so frugally, sending as much of her wages back to the investment fund in Australia as she possibly could.

With both her parents remarried, living on opposite sides of the continent, absorbed in their new families, and not particularly keen to be reminded of the miserable marriage they'd endured as their punishment for having conceived her out of wedlock when they'd both been far too young, she'd responded in the most practical way to her realisation that she was essentially alone in the world—she'd saved money.

And then the investment fund had gone bust and she'd lost it all.

If there was a lesson to be learned somewhere in this development, she hadn't yet worked out what it was. The fun-loving, live-for-the-moment grasshopper in the Aesop fable had had it right after all? The serious, hard-working ant should have its legs pulled off for setting such a bad example to impressionable nurses?

Hmm.

She did know one thing, though.

She was homesick. Gut-wrenchingly, tearfully, desperately homesick.

Bit sad that she didn't really have a home to go to. Not Adelaide. Too long since she'd first left, and the in-between experiment of a year she'd spent back there after the stints with Médecins Sans Frontières in Liberia and Sierra Leone, and before the rather crazy time in London, hadn't been enough to re-establish her roots. Jane Cheah was the only friend she missed from that time.

So she was trying Sydney, and a live-in position that offered the dangerous promise of being able to pretend she had a home. From the impression Dr Hunter had given her over the phone, she didn't think he'd do much to foster this illusion, and that was probably for the best. There were many things she liked about a footloose life, perhaps the most important being that you knew exactly where you stood.

She tried to form a picture of Dr Hunter in her mind, based on the way his voice had sounded and the things she knew about him, but couldn't do it. Even his attitude to the babies had been hard to read. She'd just have to wait.

Two days. The long flight. Then Keelan Hunter himself would meet her at the airport and take her…home?

No.

Not home. Not really. Just the next waystation.

Her stomach churned.

Ms Russell looked like what she was—a seasoned Australian traveller returning home after a long absence. Keelan had her name held up on a large piece of card, and when she saw it she steered straight towards it through the crowded terminal, looking tired, relieved, a little dishevelled and wary.

He could match her on three out of those four attributes. Tired because he'd been up half the night at the hospital, relieved because he hadn't been one hundred per cent convinced that she would actually be on the plane, and he was definitely wary.

He would try not to let it show, but the wariness would probably last for weeks. Until he worked out how this was going to operate. Until he knew if Tam would live, and how long both babies might need in-home professional care.

'Hello.' She put down two distinctly battered suitcases and held out her hand. 'Dr Hunter?'

'Yes.' He thought about inviting her to call him Keelan, but held back and said instead, 'How was your flight? This is all your luggage?'

'I've got used to travelling light.' She took it on trust that he remembered the details of her résumé, with its references to periods spent in two different clinics in the developing world, in contrast to the high-level neonatal experience he'd employed her for.

'You need some new suitcases,' he told her.

'And travelling cheap.' She grinned, inviting her to meet him halfway, which he did, because she'd taken him by surprise.

She had an infectious smile, careless and open like a boy's. It went with the liberal splash of freckles across her nose and the red-brown hair, bushy after the flight. Her eyes were a startling blue, and seemed to light up like the flash of sun on water, making the smile dazzling as well as infectious. She was thirty-two, he knew, but she looked younger.

'Fair enough,' he said, and nudged her gently aside so he could grab the pair of shabby handles.

The things weighed a ton, belying her statement about travelling light. Couldn't be clothes. She was wearing a long, modest skirt and long-sleeved top, with a wide white scarf around her neck that she would have used to cover her head in Saudi, and in that part of the world he doubted she would have needed much more than a few repetitions on the same theme. No thick coats or evening clothes or sports gear.

'I'm sorry,' she said. 'Too many books in there. I tended to hoard them in Riyadh, because they were hard to get.'

'Didn't you have someone equally desperate to pass them on to?'

'I passed on all the ones I could bear to part with.' Then she apologised again and finished, 'I hope your car's not far.'

'It's fine. And there's an empty bookcase in the room I've set aside for you.'

She frowned for a moment as if picturing this unfamiliar idea—that she might unpack her books and put them on shelves—then said, 'Something we didn't sort out before—how long are you expecting this arrangement to continue? I mean, once the babies reach, say, one month corrected age, four months since birth, they're hopefully not going to need the level of specialised care I can provide. And a full-time, in-home nurse is…' She stopped.

'Expensive,' he finished for her. 'Look, that's not an issue.'

Another beat of silence. 'No, OK.'

Keelan could almost feel the mental backstep she took as she considered what he'd just revealed. Well, it was pointless to pretend that he struggled for money. The income from his investments competed, to a healthy extent, with his salary as a hospital-based paediatrician, and he'd benefited from an inheritance as well. She'd see all the evidence of his established lifestyle soon enough.

'I'll keep you as long as I feel it's in the twins' best interests,' he said. 'You're right. That'll probably be around four months, from a medical perspective.' In other areas, it was more complex, but he didn't want to thrash this through with her now, when they'd only just met. She might not last a week, if they weren't happy with each other. 'Do you need to know? Do you have a future commitment elsewhere?'

'No, no commitments. Just wondering.'

'Whether it's worth unpacking the books?'

'Something like that.'

A silence fell, slightly awkward. He guessed she was sorting and arranging her first impressions, the way he was, and the way she might, or might not, sort and arrange this forty-kilogram load of books in her new room.

On the whole, he'd had no surprises so far, either

pleasant or otherwise—unless you counted that smile, which was dazzling. Great for Tavie and Tam, when they got to the smiling stage. Or Tavie, anyway. He wasn't letting himself count on little Tam yet.

His gut whipped like a snake suddenly, and his eyes stung. He hadn't wanted these babies in his life, and now, already, he didn't want to lose them. He didn't want to be defeated on this.

If he was going to step in, do the right thing, the thing no one else was prepared or equipped to do—even though everyone agreed that the babies must be kept within the Hunter clan—he absolutely did not want to fail in any part of it.

This, at heart, was why he'd chosen an experienced neonatal nurse as their initial carer, instead of a nanny with a mere first-aid certificate. The babies had to live, and they had to thrive. That was all he needed from Jessica Russell. Her competence, her diligence, her professional care. For around four months.

'Can I take you up to the hospital as soon as you've unpacked?' he said.

'Make that unpacked and had a shower, and you have a deal,' she answered at once.

'I'm sorry. Maybe you need to sleep as well.'

'If I let myself do that, I probably wouldn't wake again for the full eight hours, and then I wouldn't sleep tonight.'

'Right.' He had a fleeting image of her wandering around his house at one in the morning, and didn't like it.

'The shower will do. And I'll unpack later, on condition that you show me where the coffee is.'

She tried her smile on him again, but this time he

didn't respond. He'd got caught up in the implications contained in her mention of coffee.

The two of them would be sharing a fridge and a coffee-maker, living under the same roof.

His house was idiotically large for one adult. He'd inherited it from his grandfather seven years ago, when he'd been twenty-eight. He'd kept it and renovated it, but he'd been married back then, so there had been two people to make use of the space, with the vague prospect of children in the future. The marriage hadn't lasted, however, and Tanya had gone back to New Zealand after the divorce.

He loved the house too much to think of selling it, which meant that now there was plenty of room for an adoptive father, a pair of newborn twins and their nurse. He felt uncomfortable about it all the same. Babies weren't good at boundaries. Some adults weren't either.

'Of course,' he told Jessica quickly. 'I'll give you a tour of the kitchen. I don't eat at home very much, so we shouldn't get in each other's way there.'

'I'll certainly try not to get in yours!'

'Put whatever you want in the fridge and pantry. You have your own bathroom and sitting room. Anyway, you'll see it soon enough.'

They cleared the airport a few minutes later, drove up Southern Cross Drive past bevies of Sunday golfers enjoying the spring sunshine, then swooped down into the traffic tunnels that now ran beneath the city and the harbour. There weren't many cars about, and they turned into his driveway in the North Shore suburb of Cremorne within fifteen minutes of leaving the airport.

They hadn't talked at all during the journey, because Ms Russell had thoughtfully closed her eyes and pretended to be asleep. Keelan appreciated the gesture.

When she shifted in the passenger seat, arching her spine, getting herself comfortable, his skin prickled and stood on end, like that of a tomcat confronting a back-yard rival. She seemed to impinge on his space somehow, and he didn't like it.

He brought her luggage upstairs for her. Since she followed in his wake, he couldn't see from her face and manner what she thought of the house. She'd hardly be able to complain, however. It was a prime piece of real estate, with harbour views, privacy, a large garden and spacious interior.

He'd had the place professionally decorated in a clean, warm yet unfussy style—lots of pale yellow, creamy white and sage green, with accents here and there in rust and teal. There were leather couches, botanical prints, the odd well-placed antique or original painting that he'd acquired from the family. It felt like home to him.

'There's a living room, dining room, study, breakfast room and kitchen downstairs,' he told her, keeping it clipped and brief. 'A terrace opens off the breakfast room and leads into the garden. Oh, and there's a powder room and laundry, too.'

'I'll need the laundry, I'm sure, as soon as Tavie comes home!'

'Up here, there's my master suite, and everything else is essentially yours. Babies' room here, next to your bedroom.'

They both stood in the doorway and looked at it, Ms Russell poised just in front of the arm he rested against the doorframe.

'Looks as if you have some shopping still to do,' she said.

The room contained a couch, a rocking chair and a chest of drawers, and there was still plenty of space, but he hadn't had a chance to fill it yet. In a spirit of superstition that he privately mocked in himself but couldn't shake, he wouldn't buy Tam a cot until after his heart surgery. Well after it.

'I'll get you to buy what we need,' he answered. 'I've made a list. But if there's anything I've forgotten, you have *carte blanche*. Clothes, toys. I've noted all the obvious stuff, I think.'

'Do you want to use disposables or cloth?'

'Your choice.'

'Both, probably. Cloth is better for preventing rashes. Disposables are easier to change when they're still all wired and tubed.'

'I wish there was a connecting door between your room and this one. I thought about getting one put in, but there just hasn't been time.'

'Of course there hasn't,' she murmured. 'Can't imagine…'

He moved on down the corridor, seeking to escape her empathy. 'Next comes the bathroom, and then the room you can use as a sitting room. It opens onto a balcony, and there's a TV. Towels, sheets… I have a part-time cleaner…housekeeper, really…and she's set everything up for you. I can increase her hours once Tavie comes home, if you need extra help.'

'Thanks,' Jessie said.

She stood in the middle of her new bedroom, feeling a little awkward, while Dr Hunter put down her embarrassing suitcases. She glimpsed his palms, and they looked reddened and creased by the inadequate, scruffy handles. Really, next time she took off to some distant corner of the globe, she needed to invest in new luggage.

'Let me get you that coffee while you have your

shower,' he said. 'Come down to the kitchen when you're ready.'

She nodded. 'I won't be long.'

'No, take your time. I have a couple of calls to make.'

About her, possibly. To announce that she'd safely arrived, thus keeping the twin project on track.

She had the impression, after the flurry of phone calls and e-mails that had passed between the two of them, and between herself and the nursing agency, that the twins were a family obligation which had been delegated to him, and that he would have to report on any developments to certain relatives.

Sad.

Difficult.

Not surprising, though, maybe.

The nursing agency had told Jessie something about Keelan Hunter's very well-established family background, and on first impression he fitted it to a T. With his impressive height went an instinctive confidence and arrogance of bearing. With his brown eyes—not a dark brown, but intense, all the same—went a sharpness of perception that came from looking at the world from a more exalted perspective than most people enjoyed.

And with his strong body, honed from a childhood spent rowing and playing rugby at some top-flight Sydney private boys' school, went expensive casual clothes and a conservative haircut that should have looked anything but sexy.

Hang on.

Sexy?

Well, yes.

This was a dispassionate observation, not a declaration of interest, though, she told herself hastily. He had a well-shaped head and a smooth, tanned neck, and the way his dark hair was cut definitely…surprisingly…qualified as sexy. She'd never be interested in a man like Keelan Hunter on that level, however.

She wasn't that much of a fool, and she knew how to learn from past mistakes. She knew exactly what chasms of difference in outlook and history would yawn between them, and he'd been formal and cool enough to make his own desire for distance quite clear. She could protect herself with the same kind of shield.

In the shower, she felt a rush of almost painful pleasure at being back in Australia. All the little things, the tiny, familiar details told her, You're safe. This *is* home. The sound of the Sunday morning lawnmowers over the distant hum of traffic, the spring scents in the air—eucalyptus and frangipani—the way the taps worked and the fragrance of a familiar brand of soap.

She found clean clothes to dress in—a knee-length summer blue skirt and matching short-sleeved, figure-hugging top that she hadn't worn for two years—pulled a comb through her knotted hair and blasted it with a hairdryer until the bits that framed her face were dry. Then she pulled it up and back into a ponytail, slipped on some flat-heeled black leather sandals and followed that fabulous smell of coffee that wafted up the stairs.

'Much better now!'

Keelan turned. 'Yes, I can see that.' His tone dampened the comment down to the level of understatement, and he managed to hide the fact that he hadn't realised until she'd spoken that she'd arrived in the kitchen. The espresso pot still hissed on the stove and had masked the sound of her shoes on the hardwood floor of the hall.

She flashed her grin at him, and he grinned reluctantly back, then turned to pour the coffee into the two blue and white mugs he'd set on the blue-black granite bench-top in an attempt to hide the discomfort he still couldn't shake.

She was actually very pretty. He hadn't noticed it at the airport, or while showing her to her room. Now the realisation didn't please him. His ex-stepmother, Louise, had been his father's secretary. He didn't trust the illusions generated when a man and his female employee spent too much time in each other's company.

With Ms Russell's hair straight and damp and pulled back from her face, he could see—reluctantly—what lovely bone structure she had. Beautiful skin, too, despite the freckles. The shower had left her face clean and rosy, framed by the shiny silk of hair whose escaping strands contained a dozen different shades of copper and mink and gold.

And her figure was a knock-out, now that the disguising contours of the loose top and long skirt had gone. She had long legs, a rounded and very feminine backside, a long, slender torso and breasts that would comfortably fill a man's hands. Without being too tight or showing very much skin at all, her top and skirt advertised these assets quite plainly. They advertised the grace in her movements, too.

The blue of the new outfit was reflected in her eyes and reminded him again of sunlight on the sea, and he felt as if someone had flung open a window on a breezy day and let in the smell of salt water and the sound of gulls. His breath caught for a moment, and he shoved aside a surge of sensual awareness that he didn't remotely want.

'Milk?' he said.

'Yes, please, a big slurp of it, and please don't tell me

it's that UHT stuff!' Her frankness should have been awkward, lacking in class, but somehow it wasn't.

'No, it's fresh,' he answered.

She was fresh.

'And look,' he went on quickly. 'I'll leave cash in the top drawer, here, for grocery shopping. Buy anything you want, a different brand of coffee. As I said, I eat on the run mostly, but that needn't stop you from cooking, or filling the freezer with microwave dinners, whatever.'

'Thanks.' Another smile. 'I expect Tavie and Tam will limit me to the microwave option.'

'Hmm. I'll leave the menus for the best local take-away places in the drawer as well, shall I?'

They sat in the breakfast room and he offered her a section of the Sunday newspaper, as well as some sweet biscuits he'd found to go with the coffee. She accepted both, which meant they could eat and drink and read and not have to talk to each other. A sense of peace descended over the room and over his spirits, and though he knew it would be temporary, it lightened his outlook a little.

Jessica Russell seemed to be the kind of woman who didn't need to chat constantly, thank goodness. Maybe there was a chance they'd eventually be comfortable with each other after all.

When he looked at his watch, on reaching the paper's sports section, he discovered they'd been sitting here for nearly half an hour. Ms Russell's eyes looked glazed, as if she could easily have slept despite the coffee.

Where were his wits this morning? He'd intended to be at the hospital by now.

'We should go,' he said, standing up with the effort of a much older man as he felt the weight of his new circumstances crush down on him again.

CHAPTER TWO

'THE babies have unusual names,' Jessie said. 'Did you pick them, Dr Hunter? Or...'

She trailed off. Having intended her comment as small talk, she found she'd quickly trespassed into difficult territory. This man had lost his half-sister less than two weeks ago. Jessie couldn't pretend that Brooke Hunter had never existed, but she didn't want to cause her new employer any unnecessary pain.

He frowned, and as they approached the automatic glass doors that led into the main building at North Sydney Hospital, she could see that his reflection showed tense shoulders and a tight mouth.

'Brooke picked them,' he said, his tone clipped and short. There was a stiff silence, and for a moment Jessie thought he wasn't going to say anything more, but then he added in a different voice, much more slowly, 'She was sitting in a café, poring over a baby name book when the full-on haemorrhaging began, and those were the names we found on a sheet of paper folded inside the book. If she was still here, I'd have thought they were...I don't know...too odd and too frivolous, or something.'

'You think so?' Jessie murmured.

'I've been—' He broke off, and muttered something that she didn't catch. 'Hell, pretty critical of my sister, over the years. But as things are, the names seem important somehow. A gift from her. I like them now. I'd never think of changing them.'

'Mmm,' she said, ambushed by a degree of emotion she hadn't been prepared for.

She'd learned a lot about Keelan Hunter in the space of that short, palpably reluctant speech. He'd loved his half-sister, but he hadn't been close to her and held regrets about it now. And he cared a lot more about the twins than he knew. More, probably, than he wanted to care, especially given Tam's fragile state.

It was good to get more of a sense of this man and what made him tick, but that could be dangerous as well. Sometimes, in this sort of situation, you could get way too understanding, and way too involved.

The hospital swallowed them up and engulfed her in warring impressions of familiarity and newness. She'd been in this type of large metropolitan teaching hospital many times before. She'd crossed similar sprawling parking areas, signposted for visitors or reserved for staff.

She'd seen sunsets and sunrises reflected off similar tiered rows of windows in the multi-storey main building, and had imagined Nightingale-like ghosts flitting around similar original colonial buildings. These buildings still existed at many older Australian hospitals, now typically used for things like clinics and support groups. She'd also become lost in a similar maze of extensions and connecting walkways in the past.

Every hospital smelled different, however, and no two hospitals were set out the same way. Dr Hunter led the way to a lift and pressed the button for level seven, which would be easy enough to remember when she came here on her own. He'd already given her the use of his second car, a late-model Japanese sedan, and she had its keys and the keys to his house in her bag. She got the impression he didn't want to have to drive her around, beyond this first trip to see the babies, and that was fair enough.

‘Have you had a report on them this morning?’ she asked, thinking he might have phoned the unit before picking her up at the airport.

‘I was called out to another patient during the night, and spent some time with them after that,’ he said. ‘Pretty quiet, at that hour. Tam’s on a diuretic and prostaglandins, and that treatment is managing his heart condition for the moment. He’s being monitored for NEC and IVH. So far so good. I don’t think we’re out of the woods on those yet, though.’

‘Particularly the gut problems.’

Necrotising enterocolitis, in other words. NEC was a jaunty little abbreviation, or you could refer vaguely to ‘gut problems’ as Jessie just had, but there was nothing fun about the irreversible death of sections of a preemie’s bowel.

Dr Hunter, however, focused on what she hadn’t talked about—the good news on intraventricular haemorrhage.

‘Yes,’ he said. ‘Statistically, if Tam was going to have a brain bleed it should have happened by now, and even over the past few years they’ve got better at preventing those. Here we are. Let’s take a look at them. I didn’t bring the camera today, but I took some pictures a few days ago, and I’m hoping you’ll use it sometimes. Louise—Brooke’s mother—doesn’t want to see photos yet but I hope she may be ready for that in time.’

‘Just tell me how the camera works, and of course I’ll take some.’

‘It’s easy. Point and click variety. I’m not expecting artistic shots, and mine certainly haven’t been.’

He greeted a couple of nurses on his way in, and Jessie saw that here was another area in which relationships and feelings hadn't quite settled, yet, into their appropriate slots. Keelan Hunter wasn't fully a doctor in this unit, and not exactly a parent either. No one knew quite what he was, at this stage, least of all himself.

One nurse had a vial of blood in her hand, and another was racing for the phone, so Jessie wasn't introduced to anyone yet. The nurses' greetings were polite and respectful—warm even—yet remained formal. No one used his first name.

Something about his bearing didn't invite that, perhaps. He stood out here, taller than the nurses, more upright and contained than a couple of the harried-looking junior doctors moving about the unit. His stride seemed longer than theirs, and his shoulders squarer and stronger.

It was a big place. With techniques in keeping preterm infants alive and healthy improving all the time, NICUs in most major hospitals were a growth area—crowded, like this one was, expensive to maintain, busy and bright and noisy, with different staff constantly coming and going, despite the best efforts of the dedicated doctors, nurses and technicians to give their fragile charges the peace and quiet they really needed.

The two babies weren't together. Even though some studies had shown that twins did better when placed in the same incubator, there were arguments against this practice. In Tavie's and Tam's case, too, the little girl's comparative health and strength classed her as a level one. Tam was with the sickest babies in the unit, at the opposite end—level three.

They reached Tam first. He lay in an incubator, which counted as a 'graduation' of sorts. He would have started out in a radiant warmer, which gave better access to staff when a baby was very unstable and needed constant treatments and tests. Even now, he had equipment and monitors all around him.

He had a cardiorespiratory monitor attached to sensors on his chest and limbs, with alarms set to signal an unsafe change in blood pressure, heart rate, temperature or respiration. He had a pulse oximeter clipped to his foot, measuring the level of oxygen saturation in his blood by shining a light through his skin.

Amazing machine, Jessie always thought. By detecting the fine shadings of colour between red oxygenated blood and blue de-oxygenated blood, the machine could provide an accurate measurement of the blood oxygen level, expressed as a percentage. You wanted to see that percentage up in the high nineties, which Tam's was.

Poor little guy. Little sweetheart.

'Here he is,' Dr Hunter said, his voice hardly more than a growl. He didn't touch the top of the incubator. Some babies found even this stressful, and their nurses had to learn to avoid casually placing charts or pencils there, while going about their work.

Or was her new employer's lack of contact with Tam more a statement about his own distance than his awareness of the baby's needs?

'Hi, Tam,' Jessie whispered.

She was accustomed to babies like this. Most people weren't. Their dry, reddish skin, their spindly limbs, the dark vestiges of downy hair on their shoulders and backs as well as their hat-covered heads, the sheer *smallness* of them. The tip of an adult finger would fill Tam's whole fist when he grasped at it.

'He is jaundiced, isn't he, poor love,' she added.

With the yellow tinge of jaundice on his skin and the blue of the 'bili' lights above him, he looked as if he'd been stained with some strange dye, and his little nappy, a startling white in contrast, was hardly bigger than a folded envelope.

It would get weighed every time he was changed, as a method of calculating his output of urine. You wanted the right amount of fluid going in, and the right amount coming out, and with preemies you measured it all obsessively.

'Have you been able to hold him yet?' she asked.

'No, not yet,' Dr Hunter said. 'Hospital policy is to wait until he hits the kilogram mark.'

Jessie wasn't surprised, although the arbitrary nature of the cut-off point bothered her. Some babies responded very well to being held at nine hundred grams. Others couldn't take it at twelve hundred. Weight was only one way to measure a baby's fitness for certain things. In this case, though…

Tam was still being fed via total parenteral nutrition—intravenous feeding, mainly through a line into his navel. On the plus side, this avoided the digestive problems that could occur if a delicate preemie wasn't yet ready to have its little stomach filled. The down side was that it increased the risk of infection via the entry sites of the different lines, and made a preemie even more difficult to hold—so much equipment in the way.

And a baby like this would tire very easily, too, even through something as simple as being lifted from his incubator into someone's waiting arms. In Tam's case, the no-holding-yet policy was probably the right approach.

'I touch him, though, when he can handle it,' Dr Hunter added. He looked at the baby with narrowed eyes, an expert's judgement and a powerful aura of human will. If he could have pushed a two-ton rock up a hill to increase Tam's chance of survival, he would have done it,

Jessie suspected, whether he cared to call this 'love' or not.

Again, she found herself understanding Keelan Hunter's feelings more than she wanted to.

'Is he showing a lot of stress?' She kept her voice low.

Research on the youngest preemies in recent years showed that they could get dangerously stressed through over-stimulation. Their nervous systems were too fragile and immature. They couldn't listen and look at the same time without tiring themselves. When they were being touched, they didn't want to be talked to. NICU nurses and caring parents learned to read the baby's state.

'He has a couple of great nurses, who try to minimise it as much as possible,' Dr Hunter said. 'They're aware of the situation and looking forward to having you on board. Here's Stephanie now. I'll introduce you.'

He stepped away, and only then did Jessie realise how close the two of them had been standing. A draught of cool air eddied around her bare arm, contrasting with the body heat he'd given off. Thinking back, she wondered if she'd been the one to move closer, without realising it, drawn by some indefinable quality to him that she didn't have a name for yet. The force of will she'd just seen in him, perhaps.

He wasn't as urbane and as civilised as she'd somehow expected, with his classy background. He wasn't as tame or as bland. There was something almost…what…primitive about him. Primitive? That couldn't be the word. Something, though, that left her feeling strangely edgy and stirred up inside.

Just tired, probably.

'Stephanie, here's Jessica Russell, to see the babies,' he said. 'She's just off the plane this morning, so it's only a quick visit today.'

'Welcome to our unit, Jessica,' said the neat, athletic-looking woman. Vincent. Stephanie Vincent. She had some threads of grey in her dark hair and a twinkling, brown-eyed smile.

'Call me Jessie,' she answered at once, realising that she hadn't mentioned the usual shortening of her name to Dr Hunter.

It seemed fairly obvious that he wanted to maintain a more formal relationship. Wise, probably. She wasn't sure if it would be possible in the long run, however, when they'd be caring for two babies together.

'He's looking good, isn't he?' the NICU nurse said. 'Kidneys keeping up, nice steady colour. He's not awake very much. That heart's tiring him out.'

Efficiently, she noted Tam's hourly observations on a chart, checked that the fluid in his lines was flowing as it should, and made some notes about his state. Jessie watched her, aware of the baby's reluctant yet determined adoptive father still standing beside her, as rigid and solid as a tree trunk.

A warm tree trunk. Somehow, they'd moved closer to each other again, and she could feel his heat.

'Well, let's go and see Tavie,' he said after a moment, before she was quite ready to move on. She took a last look at the little boy, wishing she was officially his nurse, wondering if she should let herself feel anything like his mother.

Tam lay on his back, with his head to the side and his eyes closed. His little face looked so still, but then he twitched and grimaced and stiffened his limbs, and she knew he couldn't be very comfortable. Jessie had seen parents weeping in frustration at having to watch their babies like this, and had sometimes cried herself.

You just wanted to hold them against you, take out all

those awful lines, pull the sensors away. It was so hard to accept that the lines and sensors were ultimately keeping the baby alive.

A few minutes later, on the other side of the unit, Tavie looked a lot better, but she was still tiny—the smallest of the level one babies.

'Wednesday, we think, for her discharge, if you're comfortable with that,' Dr Hunter said to Jessie. 'She'll be done with the bili lights by then.'

'How's her weight?' she asked.

'Oh, big milestone when I weighed her this morning,' put in her nurse, Barb McDaniel, who hovered nearby. She looked to be in her late forties, with rounded hips, hair tinted a pretty mid-brown shade and that aura of experience and competence that no one could fake. 'She's hit her birthweight, 1220 grams.'

'Fantastic,' Dr Hunter said. 'That's great.'

And he actually smiled.

He blinked at the same time, twice, as if his honey-brown eyes felt gritty, but his mouth curved and his straight white teeth rested for a moment against his full lower lip, and Barb shot him a curious glance that softened into approval. Clearly, she'd been concerned about how he was handling all this, how involved he was, whether he'd eventually crack.

'Could one of us hold her?' Jessie asked.

'Do you have time, Dr Hunter?' Barb turned to him, tentative and respectful.

But he deferred at once to Jessie. 'Best if you do it, I think. The two of you need to get used to each other as soon as you can.'

'I'd love to,' she answered, and it came out sounding more like a rebuke at her employer's distance than she'd meant it to.

If he noticed, he didn't comment, and his expression didn't change. Jessie tried to forget about him standing there, and focused on the baby instead.

Funny.

In the past, so many times, she'd been the one carefully passing the tiny, swaddled bundle to an eager, tearful parent for that first precious hug. She'd been the one to make sure that feed lines and medication lines and oxygen lines and monitor lines were still firmly taped in place, yet as much out of the way as possible.

She'd been the one to give murmured instructions. Watch for this. Be careful of that. And then she'd been the one to stand back and get choked up herself at the softening in a mother's face, the total focus, the gentle hand movements.

Now I'm on the opposite side of the fence, her thoughts ran, skittish and woolly from fatigue, and from her awareness of Keelan Hunter keeping his distance—and judging this first moment of interaction, probably, behind the mask of his classically handsome face. But I'm not her mother… She's a little darling… How is this going to feel?

Warmth. That was the first sensation.

Tavie was a nugget of feather-light warmth in her arms, like a kitten asleep on her chest. She had that cheesy, salty-sweet newborn smell, and breath so light that Jessie couldn't even feel it. She had her nasal cannula in place, though, giving her oxygen, and her breathing alarm wasn't going off, so she definitely was breathing, despite the lack of evidence.

And then, as Jessie settled into complete stillness, she felt the evidence after all—the tiny, rhythmic movement of Tavie's chest expanding and contracting against her own, so faint that Jessie had to stop breathing herself in order to feel it.

She's going to live, the thoughts ran once more. Whatever it takes, whatever I have to do for her. She's going to thrive, and get strong and smiley and bright and curious, and Keelan Hunter will love her more than he can imagine. Way more than he wants to.

She didn't talk out loud, just let Tavie get used to the feeling of being held. The baby was in a drowsy state, but her little hand moved and tightened in its primitive grasp reflex, and Barb McDaniel warned, 'Watch her oxygen tube, she's going to grab it any minute.'

'Sorry, baby,' Jessie murmured, and carefully lifted it over the baby's head to her other shoulder.

'Might leave the two of you for a few minutes,' Barb said.

'I have a phone call to make,' Dr Hunter came in at once.

He would, wouldn't he? He'd have a repertoire of easy outs, ready for the times when he didn't want to get too close. Jessie thought she might be glad of this fact, too.

'I'll hear if her breathing alarm goes off, but it shouldn't,' Barb continued. 'She's usually pretty good when she's being held.'

'You've been holding her?' Jessie asked. Dr Hunter had already moved towards the door.

'Since last week. Hard to fit it into the routine some days. With these little ones who don't seem to have a mum or dad, I never know if we're doing it for the baby or for us.'

'Both,' Jessie said.

She knew which babies the other nurse was talking about. A disproportionate percentage of premature and low birth-weight babies were born to very young or drug-addicted mothers, who often had trouble bonding with such tiny, fragile infants. A distracted, nervous or uncomfortable visit once every couple of weeks didn't impress NICU nurses, who did their best to compensate.

Apparently the NICU nurses here had judged Dr Hunter in the same way, and found him wanting. For some reason, Jessie felt a strong need to leap to his defence, even though she'd seen his barriers and his boundaries for herself.

'Can you imagine how it must be to suddenly find yourself in his position, though?' she said, her throat suddenly tight. 'I think a lot of people would hold back.'

'Hang on,' Barb said. 'No, I didn't mean him. He's been in here as much as he can, from the day they were born, even when that poor, silly mum of theirs was still in the picture. No, I meant… Even with him around—I wish he was married!—they still don't have a mother.'

'They have me.'

The nurse shot her a quizzical sidelong glance. 'Planning to stick around? How long?'

'As long as he pays me,' Jessie answered, because she had to remember that this was a job, probably lasting around four months, not a labour of love with an accidental salary conveniently attached. She'd blurred that boundary once before, and still bore the emotional scars.

'So there you go,' Barb said gently, and Jessie knew she was right.

It would be a fine line to tread.

Was Ms Russell asleep?

When Keelan returned from phoning a colleague about one of his patients in the paediatric unit upstairs, she still had the baby snuggled against her chest. Tavie's eyes were closed, and so were Ms Russell's. He watched them for a moment, bathed once more in the out-of-body sensation that had become frighteningly common since Brooke's death.

Was this really happening?

Or had he been thrown back in time to the rotations he'd done in various neonatal units during his training? In what sense was that tiny baby *his*? And what bond should he hope for between the twins and their new nurse?

She'd opened her eyes. The nurse, not Tavie. She'd caught him studying her. Had no doubt seen his narrowed eyes and tight mouth.

'Just do your utmost to make her thrive,' he said abruptly. Almost angrily. 'That's all I want. If you need to leave, to move on, give me fair warning. I have no choice but to depend on you. Don't leave me in the lurch.'

She shook her head slowly, her chin raised. She had encountered angry doctors before, and there was a strength to her, radiating like fire. She wasn't the type to be easily cowed. 'Not planning to,' she said. 'I want them to thrive, too. As much as you do.'

Their eyes met, held as if mesmerised, and exchanged a silent promise.

We have two human lives in our hands. We'll work for them, and we'll love them, no matter how hard it is and how much it might hurt, because that's what they need and what they deserve.

'Barb?' he said, finding it hard to break the moment of contact and look away. His throat had constricted, and his whole body seemed flooded with heat.

The older nurse looked up from another patient's chart. These level one 'growers and feeders' didn't need one-to-one care, and she had two more babies to look after today. 'Ready to put her back?' she said.

'Enough for today. Ms Russell—'

'Please, call me Jessie,' his new employee cut in, sounding as if the issue was important.

'Jessie,' he corrected obediently. OK, yes, he had come to his senses about it now. Artificial boundaries wouldn't mean much, if the real ones weren't in place. How hard would it be to keep those? He finished his sentence. 'Jessie needs to get some rest.'

'Bub's looking pretty tired too, aren't you, sweetheart?' Barb cooed softly, and started shifting lines and moving the drip stand so she could lift Tavie back into her incubator.

They took another quick look at Tam on their way out. Oxygen saturation at ninety-four per cent. Heart rate at 150. No mottling, pallor or cynosis in his skin. Keelan searched for something cheery and upbeat to say—about the baby, his appearance, his stats—but a kind of weariness descended over him and he just couldn't do it. Jessica—Jessie—didn't say anything either.

On their way home, he realised that he was hungry, and that he should offer her a chance at lunch, too. It was already noon. When he asked, she admitted she'd been thinking about a meal. He knew of a deli-cum-sandwich shop nearby, open on Sundays, and found a parking place right in front of it.

'We'll pick up some cheese and meat, and some tubs of salad,' he said. 'Want to choose a couple?'

She picked out a Greek salad, and something with artichoke and avocado in it, and he chose a couple more salads, and bought two cottage loaves as well. She might get hungry in the night. She looked like the sort of woman who had an energetic appetite. Her slender arms and legs had a strength to them, despite their grace, which showed she kept herself fit.

He should have thought to stock his kitchen a little better, in anticipation of her needs. Tethered to the house by Tavie as soon as the baby came home—three days from now, if everything continued as they hoped—and committed to visiting Tam whenever she could, she wouldn't have much opportunity for shopping.

He set the various offerings out on the kitchen bench and they served themselves directly from the plastic tubs, then ate together, once again, in his breakfast room. He made himself ask her what she'd thought of the unit at North Sydney, and whether discharge for Tavie on Wednesday seemed too soon.

'I'd be nervous about it,' she answered, 'if I was on staff there, and handing her over to a mum with no medical training. She'll still be under three pounds, and not out of the woods for various complications. But as long as we have the oxygen and breathing alarm here, and if she has no setbacks between now and Wednesday, I think it's a good idea. I'll be able to establish a routine, give her some peace and quiet.'

'That's what I thought, and one of the reasons I opted for someone with your level of skill and training.'

The other reason was Tam.

He didn't want to ask her specifically what she'd thought about Tam. She had too much experience. She would have seen too many babies like him who hadn't made it.

Keelan didn't linger over the meal.

'I'm going sailing with my cousin this afternoon,' he told her. 'Won't be back until fairly late, probably. As I've said, make yourself at home, sit in the garden, use the car, whatever you want. There's a street directory in it, so you can't get lost if you go out.'

'Right now, I'm contemplating the chance that I might get lost between here and my bedroom,' she answered, and that dazzle appeared on her face, that gorgeous smile, radiating out from her sleepy eyes.

'If I come home and find you asleep on the couch, I'll put a blanket over you,' he said. It sounded too personal, almost flirtatious, and Keelan felt his jaw tighten.

She looked like a child about to fall asleep in her plate, her body crumpled and soft, her elbow propped on the table and her hand cradling one pink cheek. Tendrils of slippery clean hair had begun to escape from her ponytail at the front, like a halo in the midday light. She probably even smelled sleepy—warm and sweetly scented from her shower a couple of hours ago.

Keelan felt an idiotic urge to scoop her in his arms, deposit her on the nearest bed and spend a long time tucking her in.

Crushing it, he stood up. She couldn't possibly be as vulnerable as she looked right now. Better remember that. Keep the boundaries in place. An anchorless wanderer like Jessica Russell couldn't possibly be his type, even if *he* was the type who took his staff to bed whenever the opportunity arose.

And he wasn't.

He took his plate to the kitchen and put it in the dishwasher, then changed into his sailing clothes and got out of the house as quickly as he could.

Jessie heroically managed to stay awake until four.

She cleared up the lunch supplies. She phoned her mother in Brisbane and her father in Perth, and got a hearty 'Oh, you're back!' from both of them, followed by a token enquiry about her well-being and a litany of detail on their own news.

In both houses, there was a background of noise from her half-siblings. Mum had eight-year-old Ryan and six-year-old Lucy, while Dad's new three were even younger, just five, three and six months.

Her parents had been seventeen and nineteen, respectively, at the time of her own birth thirty-two years ago. She'd had a messy upbringing, getting handed over to anyone who'd been willing to babysit, encouraged to be as independent as possible from an early age. By eight, she'd had her own key and had come home from school alone to perform a required list of chores—breakfast dishes, laundry, vacuuming.

And she'd apparently been a difficult child—colicky as a baby, stubborn and grumpy as a toddler, fat and giggly in primary school, lacking in confidence in her teens.

Mum and Dad both seemed to be enjoying marriage and parenthood a lot more this time around. When incidents involving spills and fights disrupted both calls, she wasn't sorry to put down the phone.

She went for an exploring walk around the steep, crooked streets that led down to the harbour at Cremorne Point. Back at the house, she drank a glass of iced water while sitting in a jarrah-wood garden chair reading one of Keelan Hunter's suspense thrillers.

She desperately wanted to lie down on that sun-warmed stretch of lush green grass beyond the shady reach of the Moreton Bay fig, but didn't let herself, and when her eyes closed over her book and the sloping back of the garden chair began to feel as soft and comfortable as a down-stuffed pillow, she knew she had to go inside.

She would probably be keeping erratic hours in the

coming months, in any case. Best get her rest when she could.

When she awoke again, after hours of deep sleep, the house was dark and silent, and the clock radio beside her new bed read 11:05 p.m. She knew it was pointless to try and get back to sleep, and she felt starving. Was Dr Hunter asleep, or still out? Dressing quietly to be on the safe side, she crept past his room and, through the partially open door, saw his long bulk in a king-size bed.

She kept going, a little rocked by the reality of sleeping just metres away from a near-stranger—her employer, too. Did he have a girlfriend? She hadn't seen any obvious evidence of anything serious and long term. A bathroom cabinet full of make-up, for example, or pantyhose hung up to dry. What would happen if he brought a woman home? How discreet would they be, with Jessie in the house?

Still, a girlfriend would be better than no girlfriend. Safer, somehow.

As she tiptoed down the stairs, she heard him move and mutter something in his sleep that sounded like 'fluids'.

In the kitchen, she made herself a substantial snack of cheese and tomato on toasted cottage loaf, as well as tea, then considered the seven remaining hours until dawn. There was one place where other people would be awake at this time of night. The hospital. More specifically, the NICU.

She couldn't think of any good reason not to go up there again. There was a slight chance that the noise of the car reversing up the driveway might awaken Dr Hunter, but he was a doctor after all, accustomed to grabbing onto sleep and keeping it.

Different staff were rostered in the unit at this hour,

and she received some questioning looks on her arrival, but was able to present her passport for identification and they found her name in Tam's notes.

'Too jet-lagged to sleep. I'm just going to sit with him,' she told Helen Barry. 'Get to know him.'

'Touch him?' Helen yawned behind her fist, and apologised. 'Sorry, my kids didn't let me sleep today. You might even be able to hold him.'

'But Dr Hunter says hospital policy means I can't do that till he hits a thousand grams.'

Helen looked at her for a moment, her brown eyes steady.

'Yeah, but the really serious hospital policy enforcers aren't around at this hour, are they?' she said very softly.

'Are you including Dr Hunter himself in that statement?' Jessie couldn't help asking. She didn't want to defy her employer's wishes. She also wondered, as she had wondered that morning, how he was viewed here at North Sydney.

'Dr Hunter's good,' the other nurse answered cautiously. 'I don't know him that well. But I get the impression he judges each case on its merits, and that's what you need to do with preemies, isn't it? You can't tell by their stats which ones are going to do well and which aren't. This little guy…'

'Not telling us much yet?'

'See what you think. Have a look at him for a while, keep an eye on his sats and his heart, then we'll think about it,' Helen decided.

Jessie nodded and pulled a chair close to the incubator. In one corner of this part of the unit, a doctor and nurse worked over a very fragile newborn, creating more noise and requiring more light than she would have liked for Tam. Helen had draped a flannel sheet over the top of the incubator, but that didn't provide the baby with much of a shield.

His respirator did some of the work of breathing for him, but it was important to turn the settings down as low as possible to encourage him to get ready to breathe on his own. As she watched, he stirred, grimaced and twitched in his sleep, looking fussy and uncomfortable. His skin drained of colour and his saturation immediately dropped several points, while his heartbeat slowed.

Jessie took in a hiss of breath, waiting instinctively for the alarm, which should kick in if his heart got any slower. Helen heard the sound she'd made and looked at the monitors, but the figures hovered just within the right range.

The other baby's heart alarm went off and the activity from the doctor and nurse got even more frantic. What were they doing? Putting a central venous catheter into an uncooperative vein, by the looks of it, and administering urgent meds. Tam opened his eyes, flailed his arms and tried to cry, but the respirator tube down his throat wouldn't let him.

'Can we mask his incubator with something better?' Jessie asked Helen.

'Always seems it's the noise that bothers him, that's the problem. I've tried a thicker blanket, but he still does this whenever there's a crisis close by. Poor love.'

The other baby, a little girl named Corinne, with a pink teddy in her incubator, continued to give her staff a hard time. Her breathing alarm went off, but at least they had the central line taped in place now. The nurse hooked up a tiny bag of fluid and calibrated its flow rate carefully.

At one point, the doctor—undoubtedly a neonatal resident on call—flung the pink teddy on the floor with a hissing curse, and Tam's limbs went stiff and his eyes panicky. His levels on the monitor were bouncing around, and his own breathing alarm went off. Helen changed the settings on his respirator slightly and frowned at the blood-pressure reading.

She looked across at the resident and opened her mouth as if to summon him to look at Tam, but then she frowned, shook her head and said nothing.

Finally, the doctor left the girl baby alone, while the nurse quietly noted her hourly observations.

'OK, let's see what happens with him now…' Helen said, her voice more breath than sound.

They watched Tam and his monitors. Gradually, his limbs curled up and went still. The oxygen figure climbed back up and so did the heart. Jessie looked at his blood-pressure reading and agreed with Helen's silent, frowning assessment. It was a little higher than she would have liked. She wondered if there was any plan to put him on medication to lower it, as a way of lessening the workload on the heart.

After half an hour of peace, she asked the other nurse, 'Could I put a hand in there?'

Helen nodded. 'Let's try it. We won't have you hold him tonight, though, after all the fuss.'

'No, it'd be too much, wouldn't it?' Jessie agreed.

She went to the nearest sink and washed and dried her hands carefully, then sat in front of the incubator and carefully reached her right hand in through one of the cuffed ports, making her movements calm and unhurried. Tam remained peacefully asleep.

She didn't touch or stroke him lightly, but cupped her hand around his curled up legs and tiny, padded bottom and kept it there firmly, the way the muscles of his mother's uterine wall should still be doing. She didn't chafe or massage, just held her hand quite still.

She knew how to do this, but it felt different with this baby, and she had an illogical, emotional wish that Dr Hunter could be here to share the moment. Looking at the monitors, she saw a nice, high oxygen saturation and a good heart rate, both of which stayed steady. His colour was far better now, too, an even-toned pink. His jaundice seemed less evident than it had been fifteen hours ago.

The baby liked what she was doing.

Jessie liked it, too.

She responded at once to the sensation of precious life held beneath her hand, and to the miracle of technology, which could chart those small fluctuations in a heart's power to beat and two lungs' power to breathe so that someone who cared could read this tiny baby's well-being the way a healthy baby's parents could read its cry or its smile.

Emotion overwhelmed her, more powerfully than it had done with Tavie earlier today. It might have been sensible to keep reminding herself that this one could still die, that she'd be protecting her own feelings by staying uninvolved, but she just couldn't do it.

She wanted life for Tam so badly—and health, happiness, a sense of belonging and love—that she had no choice but to invest her own heart.

CHAPTER THREE

JESSIE spent much of Monday and Tuesday shopping.

Dr Hunter had told her that she was free to spend whatever she thought necessary, and he'd set up accounts at two different baby shops and an upmarket department store. At first she was tentative about it, comparing prices, telling herself that the cheaper cot was almost as good as the gorgeous one that cost nearly twice as much.

But then he called her from North Sydney's paediatric unit, reaching her on the mobile phone he'd given her, and asked a few searching questions about where she was up to. He then told her categorically, 'If in doubt, go for the top of the line. Don't compromise. I don't care what you have to spend. Please, don't get the cheap cot. I—I really don't want that.'

Family money, she knew.

Something else, too, which she understood just as well—an irrational, unacknowledged fear that if they cut corners and bought the cheap cot for Tavie, Tam might not survive. Interesting that a man like Keelan Hunter should be emotional enough about these babies to submit to that sort of superstition, that sort of irrational bargaining with God. He was complex.

After their phone conversation, she went a bit giddy. She'd never shopped like this in her life. There were such gorgeous things for little girl babies! Stretchy little sleepsuits in pink and lemon and mauve, little tops and pants with lace edges at the cuffs and sleeves, appliquéd dresses and soft cloth bootees. Even the practical purchases, like a change table, a baby bath and a nappy bin, were fun to make.

It just seemed a pity to Jessie, at times, that she was doing it all on her own. This was really a task for two people in love, who were thrilled to be parents.

The next day, Tavie left Barb McDaniel's care and came home, with her fixed oxygen tank, her portable oxygen tank, her tank regulator, CPAP cannula, pulse oximeter, nasogastric feed tube, infant weighing scale, apnoea and heart alarms. The hospital kept the baby's medical charts and notes, but Jessie had already set up a similar system to keep track of Tavie's progress, pick up any warning signs and provide an overview for Tavie's father whenever he wanted it.

On discharge, the tiny girl weighed a fraction over her birthweight, and although Dr Hunter had taken the day off, and they'd both tried to make the transition as smooth and unfussed as possible, it must have tired Tavie out. With jet-lag still mucking her body clock around, Jessie felt like a limp rag herself by the time Tavie was set up in her new nursery.

Dr Hunter had been shopping, too. A space heater for the baby's room and a thermometer to keep track of the air temperature. Enough pantry and refrigerator supplies, it seemed, to feed a large family for nearly a month.

'Because I realised you wouldn't get the opportunity,' he told Jessie stiffly, as they stood in the kitchen together, just before lunch. 'I'm sorry, I'm thinking some of this through as I go along.'

'It's fine. You didn't have a lot of time to make plans. Neither of us has.'

'Thanks for being flexible.'

'It's one of the things I'm good at.'

They smiled cautiously at each other, and their eyes

met and held just a little bit too long. Not for the first time. It had happened in the hospital on Sunday, too, and yesterday afternoon when the cot and change table had arrived, and they'd set them up in the baby nursery together.

Now Jessie looked quickly away. The spacious kitchen seemed too small suddenly, and she had to fight to get her perspective and her priorities back in place.

Tavie. Tam. Putting money aside. Making some decisions about her long-term future when she wasn't needed here any more. What was the best way for a woman to go in search of a home?

Tavie was asleep upstairs, and Jessie had a baby monitor clipped to the pocket of her skirt, feeding her a constant stream of little sounds—a high-pitched baby snuffle, birds outside the window, some rattly noises as Tavie kicked. She focused on the sounds instead of on Keelan Hunter's brown eyes.

'I'm going to bring you dinner every night, too,' he continued, after a pause in which he seemed to be listening to the baby monitor noises, too. 'Until we see how you're managing.'

'I thought you didn't eat at home, Dr Hunter,' she blurted out.

'I'm making an exception for a week or two. And I'm not saying I'll cook at home.' He grinned suddenly, unexpectedly, and again something shifted uncomfortably inside her. His smile was much more open and uncomplicated than it should have been. 'It'll come in plastic containers, still steaming,' he finished.

'Well…thanks.'

'Please, let's stick to first names, by the way. You suggested it the other day, and you were right. So it's Keelan, please. It's not that hard to say.'

'Keelan,' she echoed, and liked the feel of it in her mouth. 'You're probably right about the meals. I—' *Bipbipbipbipbip…*

'Heart alarm,' Keelan said, and bolted for the stairs, just as Tavie's breathing alarm began to sound as well. Jessie followed right behind him.

They didn't know what had happened. Something going on in her little stomach maybe. Keelan got to her first and touched her shoulder, and she began breathing again right away. Jessie switched off the alarms and watched the monitor. The heart rate bounced back up too high, and then the baby lost most of her stomach contents in a puddle on the sheet beside her head.

She seemed distressed the whole afternoon. They cleaned up the bed, changed a nappy and slowed the flow rate through the feed tube, so that her twenty mils went in over forty minutes instead of twenty. They checked her monitors and her meds obsessively—she was still on an infant antacid and a couple of other things—then they cleaned the bed again, because she'd lost another feed.

Which was ungrateful of her, because neither of the adults had found an opportunity for lunch.

Through all of this she cried, or slept an exhausted sleep during which she twitched and grimaced and forgot to breathe, setting off her breathing alarm three times.

'Let's try and kangaroo her on your chest,' Keelan finally decided. 'Maybe she'll keep her feed down better if she's more upright, and the body contact should soothe her. We're making classic first-day-home-from-the-hospital mistakes, I think, fussing over her and making her more distressed.'

'I think you're right.'

'Can you change into a top that buttons down the front?'

Jessie almost shot him a panicky look. OK, the accepted 'kangaroo' technique involved having carer and baby in skin-to-skin contact, but…

No, be reasonable, she told herself. As if he'll care. As if he'll even *notice*.

She nodded and went to her room, where she found one of the conservative, long-sleeved blouses she'd worn in Saudi Arabia. Lapping its roomy front panels across her breasts and stomach, she didn't bother with the buttons, since they'd have to be unfastened again anyway. Her pale blue bra was pretty and lacy but decent as far as such garments went. And her breasts weren't that exciting in their dimensions, although she'd had a few compliments in her time.

'Sit down, and I'll give her to you,' Keelan said. 'Ready?'

He unsnapped the fastenings on Tavie's tiny suit, managing her various tubes and sensor lines adeptly. Settling a little deeper into the rocking chair, Jessie parted her blouse and Keelan laid the baby against her chest. His fingers brushed her stomach, just below her breasts, but they didn't linger. In fact, he moved away a little too soon.

'Careful,' she blurted out, and hugged the baby too tightly.

Tavie squirmed for a moment, but she seemed to find the firm contact soothing. Jessie relaxed, loosened her hold a fraction, steadied her own breathing and felt Tavie's delicious warmth mingling with her own. Keelan tucked a cot-size quilt around them both, anchoring it in place between Jessie's back and the back of the chair.

'Comfortable?' he asked a moment later, watching them from several paces away now, his amber eyes narrowed beneath a frown.

'I could do with a pillow behind my back.'

He brought the one from her own bed and slid it in behind her, while she arched the base of her spine. She felt his hand come to rest on her quilt-covered shoulder for a moment, and then the wash of his breath against her bare neck, where the blouse was open and the quilt didn't reach. Her body tingled from head to toe and she felt that magnetism again, that strange, primal pull he'd begun to exert on her senses, beyond her power to control.

She closed her eyes, willing it away, fully aware of how disastrous it could be.

'She seems happier,' Keelan concluded. From the sound of his voice, he'd retreated as far as the doorway. 'I'm going to head up to the hospital in a minute, if that's all right. I have a four-year-old patient going in for heart surgery tomorrow, and Keith Bedford, his surgeon, wanted me to take a final look at him today.'

'That's fine,' Jessie said. She didn't want to mention that she was hungry. The sooner he left, the better.

She held Tavie on her chest for two hours after Keelan had gone, and it felt precious and right. Like this, it seemed as if she could almost feel the baby growing. Tavie's latest feed stayed down and neither of her alarms went off. She slept, and Jessie did, too, in a light doze that still had her able to respond to Tavie's movements.

She didn't open her eyes until she heard the rumbling hum of the garage door, just as the September light was fading from the sky.

Keelan came up the stairs a minute later and appeared as a shadowy figure in the doorway. 'How's it going?' he said softly. 'She looks peaceful.'

'She has been, the whole time,' Jessie whispered back, without moving. 'It's been…absolutely precious, really.

Just delightful.' A little bit scary, this sense of warm delight like a pool of liquid inside her. She'd never sat like this with a baby before, in a home rather than in a primitive clinic or a high-tech hospital unit.

Was it her fault that she'd failed to bond with her much younger half-siblings? she suddenly wondered. Could she have spent this sort of time with them as babies, if she'd pushed?

Thinking back, all she could remember was Dad's wife, Natalie, snatching her babies back after a scant minute in anyone else's arms, and hovering so suspiciously over any attempt to read to them or take them out to the back-yard sandpit that Jessie had soon given up.

Mum, meanwhile, had brought her second brood up on bottle feeds propped on pillows and long periods alone in their cots. 'Don't go in there, Jessie. I'll be furious if you wake him up when he's taken so long to settle.' And a couple of years later, 'Don't get him all excited like that, Jessie. He'll be unbearable after you've gone, and I'll never get him down for his nap.'

But perhaps she'd been too sensitive about it, and too easily put off. She could have tried harder.

'You must be starving,' Keelan said, breaking in on her self-critical train of thought.

'Um, yes, there is that,' she conceded, and he laughed.

He had a surprisingly attractive laugh, so much warmer and more open than she would have expected. Every time she heard it—which wasn't often enough—she felt as if she'd been let in on a delicious secret that he'd shared with no one else. It made her curious, in an illogical and too emotional way, about what other such secrets he might have.

'You should have got me to make you a cheese sandwich before I left,' he said.

'I was hardly going to do such a thing!'

He left a beat of silence before he answered, 'No, I suppose not.' Then he added, 'But I've got dinner downstairs now, so if we can get her back in her cot and hook up another feed…'

'Let me do the feed, and I'll check her nappy, too.'

'Do you want to pass her to me?'

'No, I can manage, but if you could check that her lines are in the right place…'

By shifting her own weight, Jessie tipped the rocking chair forward enough to stand easily, without jolting the baby. Keelan twitched various tubes and sensor lines out of the way.

Jessie leaned over and laid Tavie in her cot, brushing the baby with the open front panels of her blouse. The tops of her breasts felt cool and heavy above the edges of her bra. Straightening, she did up the blouse, glad that she had her back to Keelan. It was her own awareness that troubled her, however, not any potential signals coming from him.

'Come and eat as soon as you can, then,' he said. 'I'll set it out. How about we forget the formal approach and have it on the coffee-table, in front of the TV? We can pull out some videos, find a movie neither of us has seen.'

'Sounds good!'

Tavie didn't seem to need a change. Jessie swaddled her as tightly as her tubes and sensors would allow, then held her breath. Monitors looked fine. Face looked peaceful. Room was warm, but not too hot and dry. She'd hear those alarms again through the audio monitor if they went off.

She went downstairs to greet the delectable smell of Italian food, and found Keelan with a stemmed glass and an open bottle of white wine in his hand. 'Could you use some of this?' he said.

'Not to sound like a lush, but could I ever!'

'Me, too, actually. Not to sound like a lush,' he parroted on a drawl. 'It's been…quite a day.'

He'd bought a salad, garlic bread and minestrone soup, as well as fettucine with a creamy salmon and caviar sauce, and a big slice of spinach and mushroom lasagne, and it was all set out on the table in front of wide, brightly coloured Italian ceramic plates and cream cloth napkins.

Jessie felt giddy with hunger, and surrendered any awkwardness about sitting down to another meal with Keelan, after he'd been so careful to stress that their personal lives wouldn't intersect very much. She would eat, then retreat to her own sitting room. She doubted very much that he'd try to hold her here until the end of the movie.

He put it on straight away, as soon as he found one in his cabinet that she said she hadn't seen. It was an American romantic comedy, fun but forgettable, and with it burbling away in front of them, the wine and food slipped down very easily.

Tavie's alarms stayed quiet. Jessie forgot that she hadn't planned to watch the whole movie. The end credits began to roll just as she was wondering how that last piece of garlic bread would taste now that it had grown cold, if she washed it down with the three inches of wine still left in her glass.

Three inches? Had she drunk less than half a glass?

No, Keelan must have topped it up. Possibly more than once. He had the bottle in his hand again now, and she grabbed the stemmed piece of crystal beneath the hovering green glass rim to pull it away before he could waste another drop.

'It's fine,' she blurted. 'I'm fine with this.'

Both of them moved clumsily. The bottle connected with the glass and it tipped and spilled, splashing Jessie's hand and Keelan's knee. They spoke in unison.

'Sorry, I shouldn't have—'

'I'm sorry. That was—'

'No, it's all right,' Jessie said. 'My fault.'

While her hand still dripped with wine, she grabbed a paper napkin and pressed it onto his knee, imagining the unsightly stain that might be left on what were undoubtedly expensive trousers. The napkin soaked through, so she took another one and put it on top, curving her palm over the knob of bone and solid muscle beneath the fabric.

Keelan's knee, warm and hard. Her hand, moving like a frightened bird. Several layers of paper and a layer of cloth separated his skin from hers, but the contact still mesmerised and magnetised her.

This was the first time they had really touched.

She looked up, past his long, solid thigh and angled torso to his face, where she saw the same electric prickle of alarm that he must be able to read on her own features. His eyes gleamed darkly, and his lips had parted. She could see the tip of his tongue held between his teeth. She pulled away from his knee too fast, and the wine on the back of her hand splashed several more drops onto his thigh.

'Hey,' he said. 'Let's deal with this properly.'

For a second, she thought he meant the attraction. It frightened her, the way they could both see so clearly what was going on, reading each other's body language like a newly revealed and fascinating code. She didn't want it, but she didn't know how to rein it in.

But no, he wasn't talking about that.

To her relief.

Spelling it out could only make it worse. More real, somehow. And it was clear that he didn't want it either.

He took a napkin and dropped it onto her hand. 'There. Soak it up, then go and wash, before…' He stopped. 'It'll be sticky.'

'I'm really sorry.'

'And stop apologising. It's as much my fault as yours.'

He could equally have been talking about the spill, or about what they felt.

She jumped to her feet, feeling giddy and awkward, and had time to see a flash of relief in his eyes and a dropping of tension from his shoulders. Her whole body crawled with awareness.

In the kitchen, with the taps running, she couldn't hear what he was doing, but when she turned to dry her hands, she found that he'd brought in a pile of containers and the plates from their meal.

'I'll stack it here,' he said tersely. 'Mrs Sagovic can deal with it in the morning.'

'Oh, she comes Thursdays?'

'Sorry, didn't I tell you?' He paused in the doorway, at a safe distance of several metres. 'And I'm going to talk to her tomorrow about coming Mondays and Tuesdays as well from now on. She's very willing to help with Tavie's care as the baby gets stronger, and she'll handle the laundry for you.'

'See how I manage, first.'

'No,' he told her decisively. 'I don't want you to get exhausted. Without her help, it'll be very difficult for you to get to the hospital to see Tam, and that's too important to let slide.'

He seemed angry—trying to hide it, obviously, but not totally succeeding. Jessie had the impression that he was reminded at every turn about details in this new life of his that he didn't like, and that one of those details was her.

'Let me check the baby now,' she murmured.

'Yes,' he answered at once. 'I'll finish down here. Goodnight,' he added, just in case she hadn't picked up on the fact that she'd been ordered upstairs.

'Goodnight, Keelan,' she echoed in the same firm, distant tone.

Tavie slept peacefully in her cot in the warm nursery.

'I'm going to enjoy interpreting your signals more than your dad's,' she told the baby softly.

Moving carefully, she checked temperature, heart rate and oxygen level, and noted the readings down in the chart she'd started, adding her observations on Tavie's colour and state as well. The familiar task settled her fluttery stomach and cooled her down inside, and she didn't see anything to be concerned about in her tiny charge.

Preparing another feed and setting its flow rate through Tavie's nasogastric tube, she considered a nappy change, but decided to wait until the baby woke up.

Tomorrow, she would try a bottle feed—just a small one, so that Tavie could practise. Her sucking reflex had been weak at the hospital, and she'd tired very quickly when she'd tried to feed, but she would get stronger every day. They didn't want to keep her on tube feeds for longer than necessary.

Next week or the week after, all going well, they'd try some spells without oxygen and maybe even a trip outside, a little push in her pram on a sunny afternoon. Only a few weeks after that, Tavie should begin to smile…

In the middle of the night, at around 2:00 a.m., the smiling, feeding and breathing milestones seemed a long way off.

Jessie dragged herself out of a deep sleep in response to the piping of the heart alarm and reached Tavie's darkened room just after Keelan. He hadn't put on a robe, and wore dark silk pyjama pants and a white T-shirt that looked warm and rumpled from his bed, just the way Jessie felt. She wore pyjamas, too—a women's fashion lingerie version of classic male blue-striped flannel, with navy piping and a drawstring waist.

They eyed each other, and Jessie searched for some clever, downplaying, soufflé-weight comment.

Love the PJs.

Must get some slippers.

Is it cold in here, or are you just pleased to see me?

Um, no. Not that.

Not anything. She couldn't come up with a word.

'What's wrong, princess?' she said instead, to the baby. Her voice came out creaky. 'Jumping the gun on your next feed?'

Help me out, Tavie. Play chaperone for us. OK, yes, fill your nappy. That'll do, for a distraction.

The baby was apparently locked in a titanic battle with her digestion. She screwed up her face, then opened her eyes wide and forgot to breathe. Her oxygen alarm went off, and Keelan reset it while Jessie tapped Tavie's feet to encourage her to breathe properly again.

'Nothing serious, I don't think,' Keelan said. He blinked the sleep out of his eyes.

'No, she's just being a preemie.'

'Can you handle the rest?' He hid a yawn behind his fist.

The nightlight plugged into the wall socket etched a gold sheen onto his skin, highlighting the fine, dark hairs on his bare forearms. Again, Jessie was slammed with an awareness of just how male he was. She'd never met a man before who had drawn her with quite this instinctive, sensual power, particularly when she didn't want it at all.

'It's fine,' she answered. 'She's still not happy, though. I'd…um…close your door.'

'It was closed,' he drawled. 'And I think her cry is louder than the alarm.' He didn't leave, however. He hovered, frowning and square-jawed, clearly unable to let go.

'I'll close this one as well,' Jessie offered.

Her steps towards it had the effect of chasing him out, and he muttered over his shoulder, 'Thanks. I've got a couple of tough patients at the moment, and some decisions to make tomorrow. A case conference I'm not looking forward to.'

'Sleep, then.'

But he'd already disappeared into his dark bedroom and didn't reply.

Jessie set up the next feed, took some routine observations, changed a full nappy and discovered skin which had begun to look a little inflamed. Debating on the best approach to head off a serious case of nappy rash, she patted the area gently with a pad of cotton wool dipped in clean, lukewarm water.

Apparently she hadn't been gentle enough. Tavie shrieked, Jessie winced and Keelan appeared in the doorway again, just seconds later. He looked as if he'd once more been dragged from sleep.

'Problem?'

'Her bottom's looking a bit sore. I hate waking her to

change her, but I'll have to if her skin's this sensitive. I'm going to try a cloth nappy this time. Sorry, sweetheart, I'm sorry.'

'You're using something, though? A barrier cream? An antifungal ointment?'

She shook her head, and began, 'I don't think—'

But he cut her off. 'Surely. Wasn't she prescribed something at the hospital? Isn't it obvious that this would happen?' His tension shrieked at Jessie far louder than the baby.

'No, it's not obvious,' she answered, calm but sure of herself. Doctors often extrapolated a simple problem to its worst-case scenario. She could understand Keelan doing so, but she would resist his attitude all the same. 'Some babies never get nappy rash, and others do worse if they're slathered with creams and ointments.'

She turned to Tavie again and started folding the soft piece of gauze cloth in place, ready for pinning. Keelan stood and watched her.

Still angry.

She could sense it.

'I'll keep a close eye on this,' she promised, with her back to him. 'I won't put her in plastic pants. In fact, I didn't even buy any. I bought these open weave nappy covers—which I'm not going to use tonight either. Just the gauze will be fine. If there's any sign that it's thrush, or something else that needs medicinal treatment, I won't let it slip, Keelan, I really won't.'

'Hmm.'

He was still watching her. With her back to him again, she completed the change and wrapped Tavie up, checked her oxygen and her heart and her skin colour. The baby seemed ready to settle, and the feed was going in as it should.

Now, if the baby's dad would just go back to bed…

She turned.

Nope. Still there.

'What is it about me that you don't trust?' It came out before she could stop it. 'This shouldn't be so complicated and so difficult for both of us, should it? Don't we feel the same about most things?'

'What things?' he asked, and it seemed like a dangerous question when he was standing so close, looking at her like this, in his night attire.

'That it's important to keep our own personal space. That I'm just here to do a job, even if it's a pretty intense and emotional one. That the needs of the babies come first. That neither of us is really prepared for everything this situation might entail, because no one ever is. No parent ever is.'

'I don't feel like a parent yet. I don't feel remotely like a parent.' He pressed his fingers into his tired eyes, suddenly. 'I feel…numb half the time.'

'That's OK, isn't it?'

He ignored her. 'Like a doctor, the rest. Wanting to win against death, not out of love but because that's what doctors do. We win against death. How is it going to be for these babies if I can't care for them? Love them? Really fit them into my life? What's wrong with me?'

'Nothing's wrong.' She stepped forward, flooded with an intense need to reassure him, to tell him that she understood and that he was expecting too much of himself too quickly.

She even reached out a hand, not thinking about the magnetism between them but about giving him support and human warmth. He did have the capacity to love them. She was sure of it, having read some of his reactions more clearly than he could read them himself. Her fingers made contact with his cheek and jaw, and the magnetism was instantly there, but he flinched away at once, shook his head and stepped back.

Jessie felt as if she'd been burned.

Or as if she'd burned him.

'My marriage broke down several years ago,' he said, speaking quickly. 'One of those relationships that only works when it's fresh and new and sunny, and can't withstand any of the pressures of day-to-day reality.'

'There are quite a few of those around,' Jessie murmured. She didn't know quite where this was going.

'Yes, too many! Tanya was the one who got bored first. She went back to New Zealand straight away—she was a doctor, well situated in her career, we had no children, we could make a very clean break. I hardly ever think about her. Only now I'm suddenly regretting that she, no, *we*—I'm not going to let myself off the hook—that both of us didn't try harder, so that she'd be here now. On paper we had everything going for us, everything in common. Similar careers, similar backgrounds and priorities and goals—which was, I always assumed, why my father's marriage to Brooke's mother failed, because they didn't share those things.'

'What are you saying, Keelan?'

He shook his head. 'I don't know. Just retracing my route, wondering where I went off track.'

'I don't think you should conclude that you did. I'm not sure you should conclude anything at all at this point.'

'In my life?'

'At this hour of the night!'

He said nothing for a moment, then sighed through a tight jaw. 'You're right. I shouldn't have said any of that,' he told her.

'Well, that's not what I meant,' she murmured, although perhaps it should have been. If he hadn't spilled his tortured feelings, she would never have reached out like that, earning not only another moment of hot, reluctant awareness but also his swift rebuff.

'Look, let's agree that in future we'll have a system to this,' he said. 'We'll prearrange which nights I'll go to Tavie and which nights it'll be you. There's no sense in both of us having every night disrupted.'

'There's no need for you to get up in the night at all. It's my job.'

'No, it's a parent's job as well.'

Hearing the distancing way he'd worded the sentence, Jessie ached for him, but he'd just denied her any right to involve herself in his feelings and his struggles, so she said nothing.

'Given my responsibilities at the hospital,' he went on, 'I'm not pushing for a fifty-fifty arrangement, but I'll do two nights a week.'

'That would be good.'

'Let me know if you have a preference for any night in particular.'

'It's up to you. You have on-call nights at the hospital to consider, too. I'm flexible.'

He nodded. 'OK, I'll let you know. For now, let's both get some sleep.'

Keelan's pager sounded at 4:00 a.m., and the readout on the illuminated panel showed the extension number of the neonatal unit.

Full, instant wakefulness broadsided him like an unexpected wave and he felt nauseous as he flung the covers aside and shot out of bed onto his feet. He was dressed within a minute, knowing that the unit wouldn't have paged him at this hour unless it was urgent.

He didn't page them back. If it was bad news—and in relation to Tam, he couldn't imagine any other kind—he didn't want to hear it over the phone, when he'd feel even more powerless than he felt already.

Across the corridor, Jessie had both her own door and Tavie's shut tight. She must have the one-way baby audio monitor switched on, so that she'd hear the baby or her alarms through that and give Keelan himself a better chance of staying asleep.

Now he attempted to show her the same consideration, creeping down the stairs with his shoes in his hand, while a cold draught from the open window on the landing chilled his neck. He scribbled a note to her, to leave on the front hall table in case he wasn't back by morning, then let himself out of the house.

They'd had a difficult night, beginning with that deceptively pleasant interlude over dinner and the video. He wished they hadn't spilled that wine—and he didn't give a damn about the stain on his trousers. Her hand on his knee had been the big problem.

Driving down the street, damming back a need to floor the accelerator pedal, he realised he'd always considered his father to have a vein of weakness in him, because of the whole disaster over Louise.

Keelan's former stepmother had carried a torch for Dawson Hunter for a good two years before their professional boss-secretary relationship had progressed to an affair. Couldn't Dad have seen it coming, exercised some self-restraint and sacked the woman before things got out of hand?

It wasn't as if their eventual marriage had been a success, as he'd told Jessie tonight. It had lasted for eight years, long enough to produce Brooke, whom Louise had always spoiled while claiming, 'She's far too strong for me. I can't understand her, or manage her.'

And then the infatuation had worn off, for both parties. Dad found Louise endlessly irritating, while she was constantly getting hurt over some imagined insult or slight, often involving Keelan's rather strong-minded mother, whom Louise seemed to fear.

In his late teens by this time, and living on campus at Sydney University, Keelan stayed out of the whole thing as much as possible, with a young man's smug confidence that he'd never get his own life into the same mess as his father's.

Now, sixteen years later, he found himself divorced from a fellow doctor, not interested in any of the women he'd met socially over the past couple of years and in danger of developing the same kind of raging, unsuitable, *unworkable* attraction that had ultimately set his father adrift from family life and left his mother on her own.

If it *was* a vein of weakness, then he feared that he might share it—feared it to the extent that he'd gone too far the other way tonight. He'd got angry, he'd questioned Jessie's judgement, he'd launched into an unburdening of his inner feelings that was quite inappropriate, then he'd flinched away from her touch as if her fingers could cast magic, hypnotic spells.

He needed to get back on a straight course. He knew that. He'd gone to sleep on a very firm resolution about it. But now something was going on with Tam, and his whole body felt stiff and cold with terror.

Turning into the doctors' parking area beside the hospital, he found himself making the kind of classic bargains with the universe that ill people and their loved ones made all the time.

If Tam is OK, I'll do everything I can to get close to Dad again.

If Tam is OK, I'll tell Jessie she's free to resign, no questions asked. Before something else happens.

If Tam is OK, I won't ask for anything more.

The lift was waiting for him, and he jabbed the button hard, as if that might make the doors close faster. The fluorescent lighting of the corridor on the seventh floor seemed garish and harsh as it always did at this hour. He couldn't hear any commotion coming from the unit, which gave him an absurd and totally illogical rush of reassurance.

Seconds later, his spirits crashed again when night nurse Andrea Stanton met him in front of the nurses' station and told him, 'We didn't want to wait until morning before calling you in, in case—'

'No, I'm glad you didn't.'

'Look, he's not in good shape, Dr Hunter. His heart is failing, he's showing evidence of a major candida infection, and Dr Nguyen has concerns about his kidneys. He's here now, and he wants to talk to you about options.'

'Let me look at the baby first.'

She nodded, her face betraying the helpless empathy she'd given to desperate parents so many times before. 'Of course,' she said. 'Of course, Dr Hunter.'

CHAPTER FOUR

'THE heart is having a tougher time than we had hoped, I'm afraid, Keelan,' neonatologist Dr Daniel Nguyen said.

Keelan knew the other doctor quite well. They were around the same age, and they'd shared patients in the past. Sometimes a chronically ill baby graduated directly from the neonatal unit to the paediatric ward upstairs. In such cases, the prognosis was rarely good, so they'd had bad news to communicate to each other before.

This time it felt so different.

'Tam's not strong enough for that sort of surgery yet,' Keelan answered.

The tiny boy struggled visibly for life. He had a urinary catheter in place now, and his body was still swollen with fluid, although he'd been started on a medication to help his kidney function. His muscle tone was floppy and his stats on the monitor should have been a lot better.

'No, he's not,' Daniel Nguyen agreed.

'So what's left?'

'We treat the symptoms of his heart condition more aggressively, we combat the yeast infection, we continue intravenous feeding and increase support for his breathing.'

'A stronger diuretic for his kidneys, something to lower his blood pressure, a couple of heart stimulants, antifungal agents, antibiotics, oxygen settings turned up higher…' Keelan trailed off, extrapolating all of this into multiple problems down the track.

Broncho-pulmonary dysplasia, if Tam remained on a ventilator for too long. Eye problems for the same reason, especially if he continued to need these high oxygen settings. A brain bleed, due to side-effects from the blood pressure and heart drugs. With or without the antibiotics, bowel problems remained a possibility. And antifungal medications were nasty at the best of times.

All of this, and more, even if everything they did to help the heart was sufficient to hold it up until Tam was big enough and strong enough for the surgery he would need.

Daniel watched Keelan in silence for a moment, then said quietly, 'I've seen babies in worse shape than this one come through in perfect health, no developmental delay, happy personalities, only the most minimal long-term problems with their eyesight or their size.'

'But you've seen babies in this kind of shape who didn't make it at all.'

'Yes, I have. Which is why I called you in.'

'To say goodbye?'

'To OK the aggressive treatment. Is this what you want, Keelan?'

'Yes!' He said it without hesitation, and felt a wash of anger towards Brooke that he knew wasn't entirely fair. There was no guarantee, even with perfect prenatal care, that she would have carried the twins for longer than she had.

The thing that angered him, though, was that she hadn't tried. She'd coasted along, taking for granted that her path would be strewn with rose petals, the way she always had, the way Louise had always encouraged her to, despite everything Louise had said about 'not being able to manage her'.

Even if Brooke had still been around, Keelan doubted

she'd have known what to do in a situation like this, where to find the courage and the commitment.

Tam needed someone to fight for him.

No, that wasn't quite right. Even at this tiny size, the fight had to be Tam's. Keelan had heard nurses talk as if this was how it happened. 'She decided to live.' 'He found the strength for one more fight, and then he didn't look back.' 'She just didn't want to do it any more, and so she let go. We couldn't bring her back this time.'

Tam had to decide to fight, and he had to know that someone—Keelan himself—applauded him for it, loved him for it.

'Keep doing everything you can, Daniel,' he told his colleague. 'I'm going to sit with him for a while.'

'You're going to watch those monitor figures?'

'No, I'm going to watch him. Touch him. I—I really want him to know I'm here tonight, if that's possible.'

Dr Nguyen yawned. 'Not much night left.'

He stepped towards Andrea, Tam's nurse, and gave her some low-voiced instructions, and they both fiddled with ventilator settings and IV flow rates for a while. Tam's chart rustled as they added several more lines of scrawled, cryptic notation.

Keelan watched them at work, then vaguely realised that if he wanted to put his arm inside Tam's incubator, he should wash his hands again. When he came back, Andrea was ready for him and he sat amongst all the machinery that surrounded the baby, and cupped his hand around the tiny head, capped in thick, pale blue knit cotton.

He lost all track of time, all awareness of the other activity in this section of the unit. And he didn't watch the monitors.

Just live, OK?

Fight, Tam.

Choose life.

* * *

Tavie's thin, high-pitched crying awoke Jessie at just after five.

On her way to the baby's room, she saw Keelan's open door and his empty bed. The covers had been flung to one side in a heap, as if he'd projected himself out of them at speed.

She put up a new feed and changed the baby's nappy. Tavie's skin in that area no longer looked such an angry red, thank goodness, and there were no raised areas and no sections of broken skin. In her judgement, it wasn't thrush, or any other cause for concern.

Next, she went downstairs, but Keelan wasn't there either, and his car had gone from the garage.

To the hospital?

Where else?

The callout could have been for one of his own patients, or it could have been because of Tam, and Jessie couldn't put her mind at rest when she didn't know. She thought of phoning the hospital…actually picked up the telephone from the hall table to dial…but didn't feel it was her right. If they'd lost Tam in the night, Keelan would deal with the formalities and with the grief, and her own responsibility lay in caring for the twin that was left.

After all, Tavie remained frail, too.

Waiting for news, Jessie made a pot of coffee in the chilly kitchen, then carried her mug up to the much warmer nursery, setting it down carefully where there was no chance it could spill even a drop on the baby. She found Tavie awake, alert and quiet, with her feed still running easily through the tube that passed through her nose and throat, down to her stomach. No alarms went off, and her colour was perfect.

Seizing this ideal opportunity, she checked the baby's weight gain—ten grams, which deserved a cooing congratulation. 'You good, beautiful girl!' She gave Tavie a sponge bath, with tiny gauze pads and cotton buds dipped in clean, warm water, and went through the tiny girl's mouth care routine.

'Still awake, sweetheart, even after all that?' she cooed again. 'Can you see how tense I am? I'm really trying to hide it, little girl. Look, I'm smiling at you, giving you a big, important smiling lesson, and you don't know how thumpy my heart is. Wouldn't your dad phone us if something was going on with your brother? Or does he actually think you've let me sleep?'

Thinking she heard a noise, she paused for a moment but, no, that wasn't the automatic garage door opening. The house stayed silent. Jessie considered trying Tavie on a bottle feed, but the baby had to be tiring by now. Yes, her semi-translucent lids looked heavy… She was drifting off…she was asleep. The bottle feed could come later.

Jessie grabbed a quick shower, but the clammy feeling wouldn't wash from her skin. If Keelan hadn't called by seven, she'd phone the unit. She had a bad feeling about the way those bundled covers lay like a discarded crash test dummy on his king-size bed.

'Hey, Baby Hunter, did you pee?' Keelan heard Tam's nurse say, breaking his reverie. She glanced at the new fluid that had appeared. 'Hey, you did! Good boy!'

Keelan looked up, eyebrows raised, and she nodded. 'That's what we want.' She weighed the nappy and announced, 'Twelve mils. Wonder Boy!'

Outside, dawn had broken, and the humming sound of morning traffic had begun to build. A clock on the wall read six-fifteen. Keelan uncupped his hand slowly from Tam's head, feeling a spot begin to burn in the top of his spine.

'He looks better,' he observed out loud, sliding his wrist back from the warm, moist incubator. 'His colour is definitely better.'

Less mottled, more even and pinker.

'Stats have improved, too,' Andrea said. 'Sats are up, blood pressure's down. Prettier pattern on the heart graph.'

Keelan looked at the monitors. The figures hadn't changed all that much in an hour, but at least they'd changed in the right direction.

Tam had decided to keep fighting.

For the time being.

A wave of limp-muscled fatigue washed over him, and the rest of his life rushed back into his awareness like a flood tide. He had paediatric unit rounds at eight, the toughest of two tough case conferences at eight-thirty…

Did he have time to get home first? Sleep was out of the question, but he could manage breakfast at least, a look at Tavie and a chance to report to Jessie on what had happened with Tam.

'I'll be back later,' he promised Andrea Stanton vaguely, although Stephanie Vincent would be covering Tam's care by then.

In the car, he drove on autopilot, scarcely aware of streets still blessedly quiet at this hour.

At home, at just after six-thirty, Jessie must have heard the garage door. She met Keelan in the front hallway, already dressed in neat stretch jeans and a figure-hugging blue top. In any other state he would have struggled not to appreciate the way the outfit casually emphasised her ripe, healthy body, and the way she seemed at ease within it. Today, though, the male stirring in his loins was a brief irritant and nothing more.

The ends of her bright hair were damp, as if she'd just showered, he noted, and her eyes were wide and concerned.

'When I woke up at five and realised you weren't here…' Her voice sounded shaky, reflecting his own emotion. 'Was it Tam?'

Keelan nodded. 'I left you a note,' he said, in a voice made of cardboard. 'You didn't see…?' He looked past her. 'Oh, there it is, on the floor under the sideboard.'

The window on the upstairs landing was open, and he remembered the draught streaming down from it two and a half hours ago, chilling his neck. It had blown the piece of paper off the table.

The lost note didn't seem important right now, but all the same he promised vaguely, 'Next time, I'll…' He stopped, wondering what kind of a next time there might be. The very idea made his stomach liquefy.

Jessie just stood there, waiting for him to say more, to say something that mattered. He could see that she was too scared to ask, and that something in his face had made her think the worst. Or maybe she'd been thinking the worst ever since she'd woken up to find him gone.

And she was too close to the truth.

He didn't know how to reassure her, and rasped out finally, 'He's still alive.'

'But he's not…'

'Not great, no. I need…' He trailed off, trying to work out what he did need, which way he should move, what he should do first. 'Coffee. Breakfast.' No, not yet, even though he didn't have a lot of time. 'How's Tavie?'

Switching his trajectory to head up the stairs, he almost barged into Jessie, still standing close with those wide blue eyes fixed on him, and she grabbed his arm to fend him off.

Looking up into his face from just inches away and gripping a fistful of his sweater sleeve, she said, 'Tavie's fine, putting on weight, had a bath… Um, Keelan, you feel as if you're shaking, and I— Tell me what happened with Tam. You're making me scared. How bad is he? What does his doctor say?'

He closed his eyes for a moment, then opened them to find her still there. And against all good sense, he wanted her to be. Exactly this close. Exactly this needful. He wanted *someone* to share in this. It touched him to the depths that she'd spent the past hour and a half worrying, sweating, imagining dire things, just as he had.

Her care and concern linked them.

'Heart's failing further,' he said, 'And he's battling infection. He's on all the drugs now, all the support they can give him. They can't do anything more, short of surgery, and he's not well enough or strong enough for that. It's up to him.'

'And you don't think he's going to do it?'

'I'm not sure how to bear the wait, or my own helplessness, even if he does.'

They looked at each other again, finding nothing to say. Jessie reached blindly around to the back of his neck and tucked in the escaping label of his sweater with tender fingers. She seemed to realise how tightly she'd scrunched his sleeve, and smoothed that out, too, then ran her hand up to his shoulder and rested it there, as if she didn't know what else to do with it.

Neither of them said a word.

Keelan knew he should push her away, regain control,

go and get coffee or see Tavie or something—anything other than standing here letting Jessie touch him, console him, share in all this—but he couldn't do it.

He cupped his hand beneath her elbow, then moved to splay his fingers across her back. He felt warmth, and the even, regularly spaced knobs of her spine marching up between her shoulder blades. His gaze lost itself on her lips, which were pale and make-up free but looked so soft and full, parted in wordless concern.

He touched his other hand to her hip, felt the hint of bone beneath a firm curve of muscle and skin, and let himself settle deeper into the contact. She watched him, her eyes beginning to narrow and soften, and he could see the moment when she reached a decision—the same moment that he did.

Her palm came to lie against his jaw, and she lined up their kiss with the precision of a potter shaping the pouring lip on a jug. There was plenty of time for him to turn away, but he didn't do it. The responsibility was as much his as hers. *More* his. She was only acting on his wordless invitation and need. He knew the signals he'd been giving out.

The first touch of her mouth brought the blood rushing through him in male response. Those lips felt every bit as good as they looked, every bit as right, moving against his. The balance of initiative shifted between them at once, from her to him, and he tightened his arms around her, nudged her lips apart with his mouth and deepened the kiss until they were both gasping for breath.

Keelan stroked her shoulders, her back, the curve of her rear, the tops of her thighs, claiming and exploring each part. He felt the generous press of her breasts against him, and a slow, sinuous rocking of her hips that she might not even have been aware of. Her hair smelled sweet and fragrant, its tumbling strands silky on the skin of his cheeks and temples.

She felt so warm and giving and real, and so utterly responsive. Beneath the snug blue knit of her top, he could feel her pebbled nipples thrusting against him as she arched her spine. He knew she'd be as moist as he was hard, and that they would be very, very good to each other if they took this further.

He forgot his reasons for not wanting it.

He even forgot the babies.

He simply drowned himself and this new, sweet-smelling woman in the sensual magic of touch and taste and discovery. He didn't want to take this anywhere, he just wanted to be in it now, the one pleasurable refuge, the one piece of selfishness he'd allowed himself since hearing the news about Brooke.

Jessie was the first to come to her senses, minutes later, but even so she couldn't push Keelan away and end their kiss without a painful struggle inside.

He felt and tasted so good, like cold water for a dry thirst, like home after too long away. His body was hard and strong, every bit as male as she'd known it would be, yet he moved tenderly against her, his mouth and hands searching and sensitive, not demanding or rough.

She had to remind herself in the harshest terms that something like this could feel right, even when it wasn't. Hadn't she been through a beginning like this once before? Hadn't it felt necessary then, too? John Bishop was a very different kind of man to Keelan Hunter, but both men had called forth her empathy and her care.

She didn't stop to analyse any deeper similarities, or to look for any deeper differences, she just found the strength, finally, to twist her head and push her hands against Keelan's chest and say, 'Stop!'

He didn't. Not right away.

He didn't seem to hear her. His mouth landed on her jaw and her neck, sending thrills of perfect sensation coiling and chasing each other down across her peaked breasts, her tingling skin, into her swollen inner heat. He made a sound low in his throat, like a man protesting against being wakened from a dream.

'You don't want this,' she told him. She locked her arms straight, with her hands hard on his shoulders. 'I know you don't. I know why it's happening, too. We're sharing something, all this fear about Tam, as if we were both his parents, but we're not, and we don't want this…this baggage, this complication, either of us. I am really not in the market for something like this with a temporary employer! It's not part of the professional package on offer!'

A pair of brown eyes as hard as polished stones met hers, Keelan's fatigue and stress etched in tiny lines that fanned out from their corners and criss-crossed beneath his lids. His mouth looked almost numb.

'If you're so clear on that, why let it happen at all?' he demanded. 'Why start it? Didn't you start it?'

Her confidence faltered. 'Yes… In a way. But I was…' She shook her head impatiently. 'Does that matter?'

He let a beat of silence hang in the air, then admitted, 'No. You're right. I'm looking for excuses.' His arms slid from her body and he pressed his palms to the sides of his head, as if he could push out the craziness of what had just happened. 'I won't do that. That's wrong. I'm sorry,' he said.

'So am I. I should have known better.'

'No. It was my responsibility not to let something like

this…' He paused. 'Travel any further. Totally mine. And it won't happen again.'

'No. OK. No arguments there.' Her voice sounded thin, even to her own ears. She firmed it. 'I'll stay well out of your way.'

'Yes.'

Nothing like this had happened with John, Jessie realised vaguely in the back of her mind. There'd been no attempt to undo the initial mistake, by either of them. John had taken everything she'd offered at once, without looking back, and she'd offered it without question.

Then in the end, months later, when she'd realised what a self-destructive limbo she'd become locked in and had found the courage to leave, he'd told her that the whole thing had been her own fault—the fact that it had happened in the first place, and the fact that she was unable to follow it through.

The really hard part was that she still believed him.

Less than three years ago. She'd been old enough to know better.

'I'm making coffee,' Keelan growled, and turned towards the kitchen.

'None for me, thanks.'

Her employer paused before he reached the kitchen door.

'I'm due back at the hospital at eight,' he said.

'Yes, and I know you have a full day.'

Just go, for both our sakes.

'Mrs Sagovic should get here at around nine. She's caring, and she's pretty bright. If you think it's possible to train her in how Tavie's alarms and monitors work over the next week or so, please start. I can't help feeling… I really got the feeling during the night that Tam gained some strength from having me there. That might be—' He broke off and swore under his breath. 'You know, I really understand what the parents of my patients do to themselves now. The wishful thinking. The mind games and the bargains with God. The placebo effect, in full, living colour.'

'It's not wishful thinking, Keelan,' Jessie told him, believing it. 'It *is* important that Tam knows we're there.'

He shrugged, distancing himself yet again. 'We'll act on that assumption. We'll do this right. We'll make sure at least one of us spends some good time with Tam every day, which means that Mrs Sagovic needs to know how to take care of Tavie.'

'She's already looking stronger, and she's gained weight since Barb weighed her at the hospital yesterday. If all goes well, she'll be off her alarms soon. A few weeks.'

'Time seems to run on a different scale for Tam. I'm not thinking beyond a few days.'

'No.' Jessie controlled a sigh. 'I suppose not.'

Over the following two weeks, Tavie continued to grow and strengthen, while Tam continued to hold on, with the help of aggressive treatment and a barrage of drugs. Keelan brought home the first set of photos he'd taken, and there was already a marked difference between Tavie as a newborn and Tavie now. The contrast in Tam's appearance wasn't so encouraging.

On most days Jessie saw more of Keelan's fifty-six-year-old housekeeper than she did of Keelan himself—not surprising, since she deliberately kept out of his way and knew he was doing the same. Sometimes she could laugh about it—an edgy, cynical kind of laugh like a two-edged sword.

He left notes for her in the kitchen now, pinned safely beneath the tea canister on the granite benchtop.

'I'm going to stay right through and sit with Tam tonight. Probably until around ten. Can you get something delivered for dinner, whenever you want to eat, and leave enough for me? Thai or Vietnamese, for preference. Pizza's OK, too. Suit yourself.'

'Mrs S. is coming in all day today. If Tavie looks good, can you plan to spend the afternoon in the unit with Tam?'

'On hospital call tonight, so I won't be home. Plenty of pizza left. I'll phone some time for a report, so switch off the ringer if you're sleeping. Tam a touch feverish in the night, but fine now—6 a.m. Dr N. trying nasogastric feed today, if all well.'

When they did see each other, they were polite and careful, like new colleagues in a hospital unit who didn't want to tread on each other's toes. What a pity they couldn't have fallen into this pattern from the beginning!

When Tavie had been home from the hospital for three weeks, Dawson Hunter came to visit his tiny granddaughter. He must have arranged to meet his son here at a specific time, as the two of them came in together.

When she heard their voices, Jessie was upstairs, sitting in the rocker with the baby in her lap, attempting a bottle feed. Tavie's suck had strengthened, but she still tired quickly, and her nasogastric tube remained in place. Without it, she wouldn't have received all the nourishment she needed. Fortunately, unlike many preemies, and especially the formula-fed ones, she had a strong stomach valve for her size and kept most of her feeds down.

She had celebrated her one month birthday last week, but her gestational age had not yet reached thirty-four weeks. She no longer forgot to breathe when she got startled or stressed, but it still happened sometimes when she fell into a deep sleep.

Mrs Sagovic—getting more and more clucky over Tavie every day, and shocked at the photos of Tam, who remained so fragile in contrast—had become adept at tickling the little girl's feet or stroking her forehead to rouse her when the breathing alarm went off, and Jessie had begun snatching an increasingly precious hour at the hospital with Tam every morning, and occasionally in the afternoon as well.

Little fighter.

He clung to life, and he'd put on a tiny amount of weight—real growth, not retained fluid—but no one wanted to relax yet.

'I'm not!' said a man's voice downstairs, mid-conversation. Jessie knew it must be Keelan's father, but they didn't sound alike. Dawson Hunter, QC, had a voice like cement rattling in a mixer, exacerbated at the moment by an emotion she could detect but couldn't name. 'This will be easier. With the other, there's no point.'

Two sets of footsteps echoed on the hardwood stairs.

'He's doing better than he was,' Keelan said.

'That, I can't imagine! But it's your area.'

'I'm speaking as a parent, not as a doctor.'

'Yes, well…a parent… Dear God! How did we get to this?'

'Jessie?' Keelan called from the landing, lowering his voice.

'Yes, we're here,' she called back. 'She's feeding. Falling asleep, naughty girl.'

She looked up as the two men appeared in the doorway, Keelan's father first. Not quite as tall as Keelan, but close, he had to be in his mid-sixties, with a commanding head of grey hair, a prominent nose and weathered skin.

His mouth was pressed tightly shut and he bristled with tension and reluctance.

'Dad, this is Tavie's nurse, Jessie.'

'Hi,' Jessie said. 'It's good to meet you, Mr Hunter.' She tapped Tavie's cheek gently, hoping she'd stay awake long enough to meet her grandfather properly.

Dawson raised his eyebrows slightly in greeting and gave a short nod, then unglued his white-lipped mouth to say in apparent disbelief, 'And this is the big one! The strong one! I can't even imagine…'

'She's growing as hard as she knows how,' Jessie answered with a smile, even though he'd probably been talking to his son, not to her. The two men seemed like magnets with their poles positioned to push each other away.

Keelan hadn't fully explained why his father had been unable to put in an appearance before this. 'He couldn't,' he'd said a couple of days ago, during a brief conversation on the subject.

That hadn't told Jessie much. There were many different kinds of 'couldn't'. Now that she was face to face with the man, she suspected the emotional kind, and her heart went out to him, despite his brusque, instinctively arrogant manner…or perhaps because of it. He found this whole thing agonising, and he'd just lost a daughter.

Understanding clicked inside Jessie like a camera coming into focus—something she already knew at heart but had been in danger of forgetting. Beyond the trappings of wealth and success, the members of this family struggled with the same complex, difficult emotions as anyone else.

You didn't have to let someone's different background create barriers. If you tried, you could break those barriers down.

'I'm sorry,' she said, and began loosening the blanket away from Tavie's little face with her finger. 'It's hard for you to get a good look at her like this, and this chair's too low.'

'No, I can see.' The older man hesitated, then stepped closer and bent lower. 'I can see,' he repeated, in a softer tone.

He crouched and his knees cracked. Jessie tapped Tavie's cheek again, and the baby opened her dark blue eyes, crinkled up one side of her nose and pursed her lips, with their tiny, translucent pink sucking blisters. She seemed nicely alert, interested in what she could hear and see, even if the sights were blurry.

Keelan's father rocked forward on his haunches, and put his hand on the rocking chair's wooden arm. 'She's beautiful…and she looks so much like Brooke,' he said in his gruff voice, and then his shoulders began to shake.

He stood up blindly and turned away from Jessie and the baby. Keelan put an angular arm around his shoulders and squeezed. 'Dad?' he said, sounding at first confused, then comprehending. 'Dad…'

They were the tears of a man who hadn't cried in half a century, rusty and painful and deep. Jessie caught one glimpse of Keelan's face, appalled and concerned, then the two men left the room together without speaking, their arms still locked together. Once more, Jessie heard their footsteps on the stairs.

Tavie didn't understand what all the fuss was about. She just thought that the light patterns she could see in the window were very interesting and pretty. And she had no idea how precious and important she was, and what a good, difficult thing she'd just done, unlocking her grandfather's pent-up grief.

'There's still a long way to go, darling girl,' Jessie told

the baby. 'But your grandad's going to be OK, with you around. The two of you are going to think each other are pretty special, I think.'

She felt a wash of tenderness, and when Tavie drifted off to sleep, she kept the baby snuggled on her lap for a long time.

CHAPTER FIVE

WHEN Dawson had left, after indulging in a stiff whisky out in the garden, Keelan stood in the front hallway for some seconds, debating with himself what to do next.

He still felt very emotional, pained by the amount of grief his father had displayed and yet hopeful in a way he hadn't been before that some unexpected blessings might come from Tavie's birth and his own involvement in her life. His complex, angry grief over his half-sister's death had eased a little.

By becoming the twins' father, he realised, he might enable Dad to find comfort and satisfaction in his new role as a grandfather.

'I should have come before this,' Dad had said, as they'd stood together in the driveway beside Dawson's latest luxury car. 'I'm sorry. I'll come again soon. And I'll stay longer. Hold her, or something. Give her a bottle. I just didn't want to…in front of that…you know, the girl, Tavie's nurse.'

'I understand, Dad.'

'Do you?' He'd collected his feelings again with difficulty, and had asked in a much more matter-of-fact tone, 'Is she good, the nurse? Do you have faith in her? Because I can't help thinking, such a fragile little girl in the wrong person's care…'

'No, Jessie is very good,' Keelan had answered at once. 'No doubts on that score.'

Except for his growing doubt as to how he and the twins would manage when she eventually left. This was just a job for her after all, not a lifetime commitment. As far as lifetime commitments went, he had no evidence that she'd ever made any of those, with all those years knocking about from London to Adelaide to Liberia to Saudi Arabia.

They hadn't talked much over the past couple of weeks, of course. He hadn't learned much more about her than he'd read in her résumé or discovered during her first three days under his roof. You could view the fact that they hadn't talked in one of two ways. First possibility—that they'd sensibly decided to keep an appropriate professional distance after one unfortunate lapse of judgement. Second possibility—that they were running scared.

The second possibility was ridiculous even to consider, Keelan revised immediately as he headed up the stairs. What power could one kiss have to scare him? He'd kissed women before.

OK, so 'scared' was the wrong word. He didn't want to scare *her*, more to the point—ruin any possibility of a healthy working relationship, so that she'd leave and he'd have to start again with someone new. He sensed she might bolt, just decamp, if things went too sour between them. Her career history suggested she might have done so in the past, and he just didn't want that. Tavie was thriving. Tam was…still here.

Stephanie Vincent had said to Keelan the other day, 'His oxygen sats are definitely better when you or Jessie are touching him. I love that!'

And it was true. He'd noted those levels himself. You couldn't fake the tenderness that Jessie showed, or the attention to detail. The charts she still kept to record Tavie's progress were meticulous, yet frequently softened and personalised with little notes to the baby, accompanied by forests of exclamation points.

'Wow, Tavie!!!' or 'Bad girl!!! How come you don't like breathing at 3 a.m.!!!'—as if she expected that the baby's charts would be kept down the years as mementoes, to show to Tavie herself when she was old enough to understand.

In the baby's nursery, he found Jessie relaxed and dozing, with Tavie snuggled in her arms. The baby stayed asleep, but the nurse opened her eyes as soon as she heard Keelan in the doorway.

'Dad's left,' he said.

'It was great that he came,' she answered.

'Yes, it was.' He added after a moment, 'To be honest, I didn't expect him to break down like that. I hope it didn't make you—'

'No! Oh, no! Uncomfortable? Of course not. It seemed as if he really needed it, Keelan. That Tavie might really help.'

Unconsciously, she tightened her arms around the tiny, blanketed bundle, and something shifted inside Keelan as he took in the tender picture—Jessie's shoulders protectively curved, the baby's dark little head, the light from the window making the fine hairs on Jessie's arms gleam like white gold.

'I thought maybe you might have gone out together to eat or something,' she finished.

'No, he had a business dinner.'

'And did he see Tam?'

'No. He didn't feel ready for that yet.'

'Mmm. Sometimes people can't make a commitment to the baby until they know if the baby's committed to life,' Jessie said.

'One way of putting it. Accurate, probably.'

Keelan shifted his weight, oddly unsure of his next move. The unsure feeling irritated him. In seventeen years of successful adult life, it remained a rare experience, but it had become much more familiar since his sister's death.

Striding across the room, he pulled a second chair out from the wall and sat down. 'My turn to hold her? Can you pass her across without waking her?'

Jessie smiled. 'I think she's out for the count. She had a good feed.' She rose carefully, mindful of the nasogastric tube and the wiring for the alarms.

When Tavie was settled in Keelan's arms and still safely asleep, he asked, 'How many times did her breathing alarm go off last night? Really go off, I mean, rather than a false one.'

Those could happen often if the baby shifted position too much. It had to be tiring for Jessie, getting up several times a night to reset the device after a false trigger, in addition to running Tavie's tube feeds, checking her vitals and responding to her cries.

'Just once,' Jessie said, her face brightening, because this was an achievement for Tavie.

Jessie did look tired, although Mrs Sagovic had told Keelan that the nurse tried to find time for a nap each day. The nap must be adequate compensation for the disrupted nights, in Jessie's own view at least, because she never complained. And the fatigue around those dazzling sunlight-on-water eyes suited her, in an odd way.

'Is that a personal best for her?' Keelan suggested, smiling back.

He watched Jessie as she sat down again in the rocking chair. She kicked off her sandals and lifted her feet to the seat, hugging her arms around her knees.

Pretty feet, he noticed. Neat, soft heels and tapering

toes, painted in clear polish. She used the motion of her body to rock the chair gently back and forth. Didn't look as if she was thinking about it, probably because she instinctively did the same thing whenever she held Tavie there.

'Yep,' she answered Keelan. 'She's getting stronger every day. How long do you want to keep the alarm in place once the genuine triggers taper off to zero?'

'You're asking me how nervous I am, right?'

'Seeing if your nerve level matches mine. To be honest, Keelan, I—I won't sleep any better without the alarm's false triggers, if I'm even the slightest bit afraid we've taken her off it too soon.'

'No.' He felt a frown crease his forehead. 'And I want you to know how much I appreciate your level of care.'

'Oh, of course. Thanks. As if I'd give anything less, though, when it's so important.'

She was a study in contrasts, he decided. Sitting there with her legs curled up and her feet bare, her hair scraped back in a ponytail that needed brushing, she looked as if she took life pretty casually. Yet she'd had the commitment not only to work in the highly specialised and emotionally demanding area of neonatal care, but to take on two separate stints for Médecins Sans Frontières in between. Had those simply been passports to travel for someone who wanted to see the world?

On an impulse, wanting to understand her better, he said, 'Tell me about Liberia and Sierra Leone. What was the hardest part about working in that sort of situation?'

'Um, the infrequency of hot showers?' Her smile was impish this time.

'No, seriously.'

'Seriously?' She sighed. 'In some ways, the hardest part was stepping back, afterwards, into a world where people take hot showers for granted. And good medical care. And water. And food. The sheer *plenty* jars more when you return to it than the scarcity jars when you first encounter it.'

'And then you worked in London for a year.'

'It's what Australian nurses are supposed to do—use their qualifications as passports to travel.'

Just as he'd thought. She'd even used the same expression.

'Storing up life experience?' he suggested.

'Definitely!' Her expression was complicated, and he guessed that not all of the experiences had been good ones. Would have asked more, except that it would have seemed like prying, given the clouded look that still lingered in her eyes.

'But not putting down roots,' he said instead.

'I thought I might have done, for a while, but that turned out to be wrong.' Again, her tone and her expression suggested he shouldn't go any further in that direction—which, of course, made him want to do just that. She thought for a moment, then added, 'I don't have high expectations regarding roots, I guess.'

'No, I think I'd got that impression already,' he drawled.

She gave him a sharp look. 'That's not a problem for you, is it? As a philosophy of living, it's not something that impinges on the way I do my job. In some ways, it probably helps. I couldn't be so committed to these babies if I had a lot of competing demands in my personal life.'

'True.'

And he'd met nurses like that before. Doctors, too, for that matter. They seemed to live for their work, and you'd swear someone simply took their batteries out and stored them in a box whenever they weren't haunting their particular domain, obsessing about patients or protocols or professional politics. They could be scary people.

Jessica Russell didn't quite seem to fit that profile somehow, but Keelan couldn't put his finger on the difference. It shouldn't matter to him, in any case.

Tavie snuffled in her sleep. She was turning into a noisy baby. On the nights when Keelan was scheduled to get up for her and therefore had the monitor in his room, she sounded like a piglet or a kitten. It disturbed his sleep, but he forgave her for it because, in fragile contrast, Tam usually lay so still and quiet.

With all the noise in the NICU, the sound of crying babies was eerily absent. They had tubes between their vocal cords, they were too heavily medicated, or they just didn't have the strength.

'Is she waking up?' Jessie asked.

'No, just pigletting.'

She laughed. 'Pigletting. I like that. It fits.' She stretched her legs down to the floor again, and slipped her sandals back on. 'Want to put her in her cot?'

'I should. I have a couple of calls to make. And I'm getting hungry. Any preferences?'

She made a face. 'I was going to…' She stopped, as if rethinking her quick response, and took a breath. 'Actually,' she continued slowly, 'I was going to hide in my room until you'd eaten, then sneak downstairs and cook myself scrambled eggs on toast. I'm ready for a break from container food. Would you mind?'

'You don't need to sneak, do you? Or ask about using our eggs?'

'No, but you know what I mean. I'm poking fun at the way we've been avoiding each other. Maybe I shouldn't.'

'Avoid me?'

'Poke fun at it.'

'I guess it has had its comical elements at times,' Keelan conceded. 'But, no, I don't think we should avoid each other. That was a difficult day, the night Daniel Nguyen called me up to the hospital to talk about Tam. What happened was…' he searched for the right phrase '…out of character for both of us, I imagine. We're scarcely candidates for a successful affair.'

'No. Poles apart. Backgrounds, for one thing. Lifestyles. Priorities.'

'I'm glad you agree.'

Their eyes locked, and they both understood that there was one area in which they weren't poles apart and hadn't acted out of character three weeks ago. The chemical attraction between them remained, volatile and intriguing, even while it was unwanted and uncomfortable.

'So,' he went on. 'Scrambled eggs. Want to make some for me?'

'Bacon on the side? Grilled tomatoes and mushrooms? Toast triangles?'

'Sounds great.'

'You go and make your phone calls, then, Keelan.'

'I'll open some wine, and we can eat outside. It's early, and it's warm.'

She'd had evenings like this with John many times, Jessie remembered half an hour later as she and Keelan sat on the stone-paved rear terrace, with steaming plates and chilled white wine in front of them.

Deceptively beautiful evenings, those London ones had seemed—innocent and romantic and poignant.

But in the cold light of day they hadn't been any of those things.

She'd taken on a private nursing assignment while

looking around for something in the hospital system, and she hadn't minded that it had been very different work to what she'd done in the past. She'd ended up staying with them quite a bit longer than originally planned.

During that summer, she would spend long days nursing John's wife Audrey at home while John was at work, running his successful management consultancy. By eight or nine in the evening, Audrey would be lying in a restless, medicated sleep upstairs. Jessie would have spent the previous hour fussing around in the kitchen, eagerly planning to spoil John with a delicious, private meal. More often than not, he would get home late, just as she was beginning to abandon hope.

'Business drinks. Mind-numbing. Sorry, my darling. And you've cooked? Audrey's asleep?'

Having been stricken with multiple sclerosis sixteen years earlier, Audrey had endured her worst exacerbation phase during the four months Jessie had nursed her. From her first days in the Bishops' employ, Jessie's heart had gone out to both of them. To Audrey because of what she suffered with so little complaint, and to John because he was heroically, stoically committed to a marriage which, he'd made clear, could no longer provide him with companionship or stimulation…or sex.

And he'd milked and manipulated Jessie's empathy from the first.

Why had she taken so long to see it?

He was good at manipulation, but she blamed her own naïvety and idealism and woolly principles more.

'Not as hungry as you thought?' Keelan's question cut across her thoughts, and she realised she'd been too deeply locked in memories to eat properly.

'Just as hungry as I thought,' she answered, obediently

heaping bacon and tomato onto her fork. 'Just savouring the evening, taking my time, because it's so nice.'

Too nice.

Like London.

They had Tavie's monitor on the wrought-iron table in front of them, but she was quiet at the moment. Keelan was quiet, too, apparently in the same sort of thoughtful mood as Jessie was. The way he sat opposite her, and so close, it was hard not to be aware of him. He half filled her field of vision every time she looked up.

Physically, he'd become so familiar to her now. The shape of his head, as smooth and regular as a classical sculpture, with its straight Grecian nose. The colour of his skin, a light, even-toned olive. The muscular mass of his torso, not over-developed but impressive all the same, because he sailed and swam. The way the dark hairs softened the contours of his forearm.

It would be very easy just to keep looking, to remember the way he'd felt against her body, to imagine how it might feel to be in his arms again, skin to skin, to crave his woody, living, masculine scent in her nostrils.

Music drifted to their ears from the compact disc Keelan had put on inside the house. Some folky, Celtic thing. Jessie didn't know what it was, but she liked it. The Sydney spring evening felt like a summer evening in suburban London, warm and green and filled with birdsong.

The Bishops had had a beautiful home, and with no children in their lives it had always looked perfect, filled with antiques and works of art and surrounded by a manicured garden perfumed by flowers. Jessie had assumed at first that John's consultancy must be very successful indeed, but she'd later learned that the real money had been Audrey's, inherited just after she and John had married.

Jessie had also come to understand that John's affair with herself hadn't been his first, and hadn't been the momentous, miraculous bonding she'd believed it to be, but only the latest in a long string, with some strands in that string running parallel.

Many women fell for the vibes John put out, and for his subtle allusions to the fact that his marriage was an empty shell, that Audrey's life would not be long and her death a merciful release. Tragically, he would someday be free to marry again. In the meantime…

'You can't know how much this means to me,' he told Jessie, more than once. 'To have you here, to know how much you care. God knows, I'd never do anything to hurt Audrey. She must never know about us, and I can't make you any promises. Not yet. It's a poor bargain for you. For me, it's everything.'

Hmm.

What an idiot I was.

She hadn't come to her senses, or rediscovered her principles, until she'd found the evidence of another love interest in John's life—convenient to act upon, thanks to the many business trips he'd taken. She'd played the wronged, cheated woman in a horrible emotional scene, and he'd been derisive in response to her naked hurt.

Wake up and smell the gravy, Jessie.

Surely Audrey was the only woman who had any right to complain about his fidelity? he pointed out, his urbane, civilised logic as slippery as eel skin. Wasn't there a teeny-weeny double standard going on here?

Although Jessie didn't buy that argument, she knew she was in no position to take the moral high ground.

How could she have suffered such a disastrous loss of perspective?

She left a week later, racked with guilt when Audrey told her, in her effortful, indistinct speech, 'I'll miss you. You've been the best.'

Never, never, never again.

Never fall for a man because his troubles make him seem like a hero. Never take him at his own valuation. Keep your ideals and your empathy for your work.

John had risked nothing, and had lost nothing. Like Keelan, he was too well set up in life to be cast adrift when an ill-advised relationship failed. For someone in her own situation, Jessie understood now, the risks were much greater. She hadn't had a lot to begin with. Not much money. Not much security. Not many close emotional ties. At the end of the wrong affair, she could lose even the little that she had.

'Is there any season of the year when Sydney isn't beautiful?' she asked Keelan quickly, struggling to pick up a conversational thread. She didn't want to dwell on the past.

'When it's raining,' he answered. 'Which can happen in any season, so I haven't really answered your question.'

'When it's raining,' she echoed.

It had rained a lot in London.

She finished her meal quickly after this, and although she accepted his offer of decaf coffee, she took it up to her sitting room and drank it while reading a book—one of those he'd commented on—from her suitcase. She'd unpacked them and arranged them on the bookshelves in her bedroom, but that had probably been a mistake. She should have left them in storage, to emphasise the transience of her life here.

* * *

Two weeks after Dawson's first visit to Tavie, he came again, in the middle of the day. Keelan was held back at the hospital, and Mica Sagovic had gone grocery shopping, so it fell to Jessie to usher him in and play hostess.

For a man of his position, he seemed awkward and lacking in confidence, and Jessie understood that she was probably seeing a side to him that few others had ever seen, and that the man himself might not have known he possessed until recently.

'Tea or coffee?' she offered at once, then after a sideways glance she added, 'Or something stronger?'

While looking distinctly tempted by the 'something stronger', he settled for coffee, and she suggested, 'Why don't I take you upstairs so you can see Tavie, and I'll bring the coffee up to you in a few minutes when it's ready?'

'Oh. Yes. Is she awake?'

'Not right now.'

'I thought you might bring her down.'

'We tend not to do that. It's still awkward to move her, although we're hoping she'll come off tube feeds and oxygen next week, and then it'll be easier.'

'Right.'

Jessie led the way upstairs, aware of Mr Hunter following her. Her neck prickled, and she felt unexpectedly emotional—the safe, generous yet distant form of tenderness that she should have felt for John Bishop, and should feel now for Keelan. She really wanted this second meeting between grandfather and granddaughter to go well.

When they reached the baby's room, Tavie was awake and beginning to fuss, and Keelan's father said, 'Oh. What does that mean? Is she hungry?'

'I expect so. And bored. She's starting to want a bit of entertainment now.'

Jessie thought for a moment. Tavie had begun to be weaned off the supplemental oxygen for set periods each day. She took half her feeds by mouth. It would be possible…

'Since she's awake,' she added, 'would you like to help me with a milestone for her? Her first trip outside? We could take her into the back garden.'

'Would that be safe? If you haven't done it before…' He looked around the room as if it was a fortress that only just managed to keep hidden dangers at bay.

Two weeks ago, he'd only submitted to a three-minute visit before fleeing. This time Jessie was determined to keep him longer, and to make the interlude more rewarding for both the man and the baby.

'I think I've been waiting for the right moment.' She touched his arm briefly. 'It would be a celebration, don't you think?'

'I'm in your hands,' he answered gravely. 'If you know what to do with all this equipment.'

'We can leave most of it behind for a short period,' she assured him.

He stood back and watched while Jessie detached the lengths of tube and wire. She thought of giving him Tavie to carry downstairs but guessed the idea would terrify him. Tavie had her new, unused pram sitting in the little storage room beneath the stairs. If Dawson could bring that outside for her, they could put Tavie in it and park her under a shady tree, safely bundled in blankets. She'd love it.

'This much effort,' Keelan's father murmured at one point, when Jessie had had to send him back upstairs for a lambskin to pad the pram with. 'Is it worth it?'

'It'll be lovely,' she answered confidently.

And it was.

Jessie settled Tavie in the pram and left her in her grandfather's care while she made the coffee and found some biscuits to go with it. Waiting for the liquid to drip through the filter, she tiptoed to the back door to see how they were getting on, and saw that he'd positioned his chair right beside the pram.

He had his eyes fixed on the tiny girl, who gazed up at the moving patterns of the green leaves, waving her little hands around excitedly, as if she thought she might catch one.

Way too much to read into a seven-week-old preemie's random arm movements and blurry gaze, but Jessie knew she wasn't reading too much into the body language that Dawson Hunter displayed. He found his granddaughter fascinating, and she'd brought him to a level of contemplation and stillness that he would rarely achieve in the rest of his busy, high-profile life.

When Jessie appeared with the coffee and biscuits, Dawson shifted his chair several inches away from the baby's pram, as if he'd been caught out in some sinful display, sitting so close, watching so intently. She didn't comment, just handed him the cup and saucer with a smile and offered the biscuits a short while later.

'Tam's getting a little stronger,' she told him.

'Keelan says his heart may yet give out before he's strong enough for the surgery.'

'His doctors are walking a knife edge with the timing,' Jessie agreed. 'It's been a battle to get his infections under control. Tam needs us to be hopeful, I always think.'

'New Age mumbo-jumbo,' the older man growled. 'It would have been better to let him go. To spare all of us this nightmare.'

He passed the back of his hand across his forehead, as if brushing away a fly. Jessie pretended not to notice. Tavie started fussing. 'She's ready for her bottle. I'll go and warm it up.'

'What about the tube?' The business end of it was still taped to Tavie's face and threaded up through her nose and down into her stomach, although Jessie had detached and capped the other end.

'She likes the bottle better now. Doesn't like the tube one bit. We're holding our breath because a couple of times she's looked as if she was trying to pull it out.'

'She couldn't do that!'

'Some NICU people say that if a baby is strong enough to pull out the tube, she's strong enough to do without it. Would you like to give her the bottle?'

'I could give it a try. I was never much of a hands-on parent.'

'Second chance, then,' Jessie suggested lightly, then realised that her comment had far more meaning than her tone had conveyed, in the light of his daughter's recent death. She winced inwardly.

I'm usually more tactful than that!

But Keelan's father seemed to take her words differently. 'Yes, I've been extraordinarily lucky,' he said soberly. 'I'm only just beginning to understand that.'

Jessie left him alone with Tavie again while she mixed and warmed the forty mils of special preemie formula that the baby could now manage at one feeding session. She brought some pillows to help Mr Hunter and his granddaughter get comfortable together in the outdoor chair.

Keelan appeared on the terrace while she was still helping his father and Tavie get their positioning right.

'Starting to wonder where everyone had got to,' he said. 'Dad, I'm glad you got here. Sorry I was held up.'

'We've been managing pretty well,' his father said. 'Haven't we, Jessie?'

'Very well. Her first trip into the open air, Keelan, and she loves it. I knew she would.'

She saw him take in the fact that his father had the baby on his lap, bottle included, and couldn't help deliberately seeking eye contact to telegraph her satisfaction. She raised her eyebrows at Keelan and gave a tiny nod that said, Isn't he doing well?

Keelan nodded back, and mouthed, 'Thanks.' And just that one, tiny, secret communication between them, that warm, short connection with his dark eyes, was enough to shatter any illusion on her part that she'd kept her attraction to him under control over the past few weeks.

She hadn't. It had only grown.

Any further along this path, and she'd be a mess.

No, thank you. I'm not going there again.

She flashed her gaze down to the baby instead, and watched the tiny, singing stream of bubbles rising against the bottle's clear plastic sides.

CHAPTER SIX

'YES, of course I'd like you to come and see Tam, Dad, but I'm not going to push,' Keelan told his father.

'No, well, once he's home, all right? I don't like hospitals.'

'He won't be home for a while yet. Christmas if he's lucky.'

'We'll see.'

Not for the first time, they seemed to be having the most important conversation of the day while standing next to Dawson's car in the driveway, driver's side door hanging open, when they'd supposedly already said goodbye.

This didn't score as a coincidence, Keelan was sure. Unconsciously, Dad did it on purpose. At the last moment, he got up half the necessary courage—enough to ask the hard question, while still hoping he could run away from the answer by jumping behind the wheel and gunning the engine up the street.

Simple honesty was the best response to this strategy, Keelan had decided. He wondered, sometimes, if successful men of his own generation were as startling a mix of strength and weakness as were successful men of his father's age. He thought perhaps they weren't, that there had been some progress, some balance achieved. He hoped so.

Another car approached down the quiet street. Looking up, he recognised his mother's blue Volvo and the silhouette of her neatly coiffed head. His heart lurched sideways, and he almost elbowed his father out of the way so he himself could take the vehicular escape route Dad had been looking for. So much for emotional progress…

My lord!

His parents—his bitterly divorced parents—were about to encounter each other, out of the blue, for the first time since their very precisely choreographed and ultra-polite meeting at his own wedding to Tanya nine years ago. He'd had no idea that Mum was coming down today.

He froze.

Dad hadn't seen Mum yet. She parked under a tree on the opposite side of the street, a little further up the hill, and started across towards them, waving cheerfully. Apparently she hadn't recognised Dad's car, and he'd slid into the driver's seat now, masked from her view by the glare of the sun on his windscreen.

'Surprise!' she trilled, smiling, still some metres away. 'Love, I didn't want to tell you that I was coming. Just in case. Because there's been this kerfuffle over—' She broke off suddenly, her eyes fixed on the red Mercedes, and added in a very different tone, 'Dawson!'

'Susan,' he growled back, and slid awkwardly from the car into a standing position again.

Neither of them said anything further, and neither of them took their eyes from each other's face. Keelan seriously contemplated pushing past his father, sliding into the driver's seat of the Mercedes, turning the key that was still in the ignition and getting the hell out of the situation.

He restrained himself and broke the ice with the scintillating word, 'Well…'

As the wronged partner in the long-ended marriage, Mum had the right to her son's loyalty and the right to snub her ex-husband to an extent limited only by her imagination. Typically, though, she didn't. Instead, after a yawning pause, she reached out a rather shaky pair of hands, gripped the man's shirtsleeves and hugged him.

'Oh, Dawson, I'm so sorry.' Her voice shook, too. 'I can only imagine how these past weeks have been for you. For Louise, too.'

'Hasn't been easy,' he said, that gravelly gruffness filling his tone. 'I haven't spoken much to Louise.'

'No…'

'I think Phillip has been very good. And his girls.' Louise had two stepdaughters, since her recent remarriage, aged in their mid-twenties.

'I'm glad.'

Keelan's parents let each other go, slowly.

His mother went on, 'Are you coming or going, Dawson?'

'Going. She's absolutely beautiful, Susie. It's good of you to take an interest.'

'Take an interest?' Her eyes blazed. If she'd been a cat, you could have seen her fur standing on end. 'Dawson Hunter, she's…my…granddaughter!'

Keelan's scalp tingled at the implacable rebuke in those five words.

His father looked unutterably shocked. 'But—'

'My son has adopted her. That makes her his daughter. My granddaughter. Yours, too, of course. And Louise's. But mine just as much. Never, ever think otherwise, Dawson.'

'My God, Susan, of course, if that's the way you see it, and the way you feel…'

'It is. Keelan, can we go inside? Let's not keep your father standing here when he wants to get on his way.

I'm sure we'll see more of each other now, Dawson. I...uh... That'll be...interesting, won't it?'

Keelan's father could manage only the briefest of nods. Keelan ushered his mother inside, but when he looked back, before closing the front door, he saw that Dawson still sat motionless behind the wheel, as if he didn't have the co-ordination skills to start the engine.

'She'll be asleep, and tired out. It's a pity. You just missed her first experience of the big, wide world.'

Laying Tavie back in her cot, Jessie heard Keelan's voice in the front hallway and wondered who he had with him now.

'I'm staying for several days,' said a female voice.

'Here?'

'If you'll have me, dear. I wanted to let you get settled before I came down, to give you time to, well, start feeling like a parent, but now I'm feeling selfish and I couldn't wait any longer to see her properly. So will you have me?'

'Of course I'll have you, but you might prefer better accommodation than I can offer. There's no spare room any more. Tavie has her nursery, and I've given Jessie a bedroom and a sitting room.' Keelan's voice got closer as he spoke.

Keeping her curiosity down to a simmer, Jessie set up the alarms again and clipped the pulse oximeter to Tavie's foot. Ninety-eight per cent, the monitor indicated, which was great after the baby had been breathing regular air for a whole hour with no respiratory support.

'You are so good and strong, little girl,' she told the baby, even though she'd fallen asleep.

'Jessie, my mother's here,' Keelan said, from the doorway. 'She had some strange idea that it would be more ''convenient'' if she didn't tell us she was coming. Convenient for whom, I'm not sure, but anyhow here she is.'

'With a very warm, thoughtful introduction from my son,' said a trim-figured woman of about sixty. She had Keelan's dark eyes, and they twinkled, framed by beautifully tinted light brown hair. 'It's good to meet you. I've heard all the right things.'

'Um, tell me what those are, and I'll be flattered, shall I?' Jessie murmured, softening the cheeky response with her tone. Keelan had set up this mood, and his mother had followed through, but Jessie wasn't sure if she was allowed to join in.

'Keelan, have a look out the front and tell me if your father has left yet,' Susan Hunter murmured. 'He acted as if I'd kneecapped him with the granddaughter thing. I don't know why he thought I'd feel differently.'

'Some women would have.'

'And deprived themselves of a grandchild?' She caught sight of the baby, still dwarfed by the expanse of the cot mattress, and bundled in a white cotton blanket. 'Oh, and she's gorgeous! Oh, she is! So much bigger and stronger than the first time I saw her! I don't want to hold her, she's asleep, but, oh, I wish I could!'

Keelan stepped back into the corridor and went to the landing, where the window looked out onto the street. Coming back a few seconds later, he reported, 'Dad's still there.'

'Well, he's not my responsibility,' Keelan's mother said, sounding very firm about it.

Jessie got the impression, however, that at some level Susan felt he still was. Possibly, she even wanted him to be.

'Well, she *was* screaming, Dr Hunter,' the A & E nurse said in an apologetic tone, 'until two minutes before you got here.'

Her gesture presented a tranquil tableau of mother and toddler looking at each other as if not at all sure what to do next. No one was crying. No one appeared to be in pain, although the little girl did look rather pale and wrung out.

Keelan approached the bed in the paediatric section of the emergency department, and got an apology from the mother as well. She was in her early forties, rather tired-looking, but with a pretty face and Snow White colouring that her little daughter also shared.

'I'm sorry, she seems fine now.' The mother smiled and spread her hands. 'I do tend to panic with her a bit, because of her having Down's. She started screaming at home, and then she stopped, and then she screamed again and I brought her straight in. We're not far. She's hard to interpret sometimes, and she only has a couple of words. She'll be two next month. I guess she just got herself into a state, or ate too fast, or— But she really did seem to be in such a lot of pain!'

'Hang on, we won't let her off the hook just yet, now that I'm here,' Keelan said.

The child had shown some other symptoms, according to a report from the resident who'd examined her—rigid, tender abdomen, low blood pressure, flaccid body; pale, septic and very sick appearance, as well as the strong evidence of serious pain that her mother had mentioned.

He examined the little girl. She had several classic Down's traits—a flattened head, a slight heart murmur which her parents had been told was minor—and seemed like a lovable and loving child. Loved, too.

'She's our only one,' the mother said, still apologetic. 'I do panic.'

With reason this time. Without warning, little Laura stiffened and began to scream again, in severe and unmistakable pain. Tears streamed down her cheeks and her mother could do nothing to console her.

'Let's have another look at her BP,' Keelan murmured, and sure enough it had dipped again. 'I think she probably has an intussusception,' he said. 'A sort of telescoped segment of the intestine. It'll pouch into the adjacent intestine, and while it's happening it's very painful. Then it'll push out again and everything seems fine. You'd swear they've forgotten all about it, and nothing's wrong.'

'So you're saying…' The mother frowned, waiting for the other shoe to drop, hugging her child and soothing her. Experience with a Down's baby had taught her never to take good news for granted.

'It does mean surgery,' he had to tell her. 'Straight away, so that she doesn't have to go through many more bouts of this. That vulnerable segment of the intestine will have to be taken out. But it's not a complex operation, and you should have no ongoing problems. It's very rare to find this condition in a child over two.'

'So it's not related to the Down's, or—or indicative of any other problem, or something we'll have to watch for…'

'She should be absolutely fine, Mrs Carter. I'll arrange a bed for her upstairs and talk to the surgeon straight away.'

The surgery didn't take long to set up, and there were no more children in the emergency department that Keelan needed to see. He looked at his watch. If he could get out of here before someone else collared him, he could manage a side trip to the NICU on the way back to his own unit. Jessie would probably be there at this time of day.

He tried not to think of this as an added inducement, but knew he was kidding himself.

He could give himself a mental pep talk about it.

He should!

Having given himself numerous such talks over the past few weeks, he had the lines down by heart and could play them in his head like a tape. He could also choose to visit Tam this afternoon, instead of right now, by which time Jessie would be home again with Tavie. That way, she wouldn't be a distraction.

Or he could just forget the avoidance strategies and enjoy the pleasure of her company.

Why didn't the two of them launch into a hot affair, in fact?

They were both single, sensible adults, and they were living under the same roof, with all the privacy they needed, and a king-size bed. The attraction existed on both sides. His senses told him this, not any particular arrogance about his male magnetism. And yet he was pretty convinced that if he tried to get her into bed, she'd turn him down. A large part of her wouldn't want to, but she'd do it anyway.

Because…?

She had more self-control. She had a clearer perception of their differences, and of all the ways in which a relationship between the wrong people could turn sour. She'd been bitten before, and she'd be twice as shy this time around.

Pick one answer. Pick all of them.

She was probably right.

He sighed through the corner of his mouth and hit the

lift button for the seventh floor. Saw her as soon as he got halfway into the unit, and all the tension and awareness and intuition between them flooded back into the air again.

'Hi,' she said. She smiled, then looked away too quickly, the turn of her head a little giddy and the angles of her body self-conscious.

'How's he looking today?' Keelan asked her, wondering if he betrayed as much as she did with his body.

What did Jessie pick up? What did other people see? It shouldn't hit them this hard when they saw so much of each other. Familiarity should have rubbed off some of the heady, unsettling glow after nearly three months.

But it hadn't. The glow only got worse.

Stephanie had Tam's chart resting on top of the respirator while she added some notes, but glanced at all three of them when she heard Keelan's question. She made a little sound with her tongue and her teeth that he didn't like.

'He's hanging in there,' Jessie answered. 'Struggling a bit. I don't want to say that. Do I, Tam, sweetheart? But he is. The weight's not going on the way we want. Slowed to a standstill this week—you looked at his numbers yesterday, didn't you?'

Keelan nodded. Today was Thursday, and he'd had a busy week. He'd barely managed to see the baby and he felt out of touch, remorseful and newly anguished about Tam's slight but definite downturn over the past few days, as if his necessary preoccupation with his own patients was to blame.

In contrast, Tavie's health had gone from strength to strength. After Keelan's mother's visit, Jessie had steadily weaned the little girl onto longer and longer intervals of breathing room air, and bigger and bigger mouth feeds. Tavie had conformed to the unwritten preemie rule about readiness for oral feeds, and had finally pulled out her nasogastric tube one day.

During the three days that followed, Keelan and Jessie had debated whether they might need to put it back in. If she fell asleep during too many of her bottle feeds and couldn't finish them... If her weight gain slowed or stalled...

No, thanks, Tavie had told them very clearly, via her stats and her observations and her behaviour. I hate the tube. And I can handle this. See, I'm staying awake because this sucking stuff feels very nice, and I'm still growing. Probably a good idea if you keep me on the breathing alarm at night for a bit longer, though.

Keelan's mother had been absolutely captivated and had stayed for four nights. She and Jessie had got on well. They'd kept certain boundaries in place, but the boundaries were friendly ones.

'Come for a visit with Tavie as soon as she's strong enough,' Susan had begged Keelan, on the morning of her departure, a month ago now. 'And bring Jessie to share the load. She'll need a change of scene soon. You couldn't have asked for a better carer for the baby.'

The invitation still hovered in the back of Keelan's mind, but he hadn't planned a time to take his mother up on it yet.

'And he's retaining fluids again,' Jessie finished. Her hand rested lightly and protectively on top of Tam's incubator. 'Dr Nguyen increased the diuretic this morning.'

'Is he around?'

'Parent conference,' Stephanie put in, using a tone that conveyed too much. Shut away in the privacy of the unit's tiny conference room, some baby's parents were getting bad news.

Meanwhile, the flurry of nervous yet happy activity at the far end of the unit told Keelan that a different set of parents would be leaving with their baby in a few minutes. Home. Healthy. Safe.

A wave of sick envy poured down on him, tightening up his throat, making blood beat in his head, and for the hundredth time he thought, And every day there are parents feeling like this, getting torn apart like this. It's horrible. And there's nothing to do but suffer it…

'Yikes, Ethan!' another nurse suddenly exclaimed behind him. 'Are you just trying to scare me, or—? No, you're for real! You're not supposed to do this! And not this fast! *Yikes*!'

Keelan whipped around, his whole body yanked like a marionette by the urgency in her tone. Stephanie asked with the same urgency, 'Get a doctor?'

'Who's around?'

Keelan zapped his focus across the unit, seeking to answer this question for himself. He already knew that Daniel was in conference with those poor parents. Dr Cathy Richler should be here… Yes, but fully involved in a procedure on another very ill baby. Residents? Busy or absent. Even doctors needed bathroom breaks and occasional nourishment.

'What's going on?' he asked the other nurse. Carol something. He didn't waste time checking her badge. Should know her last name, but it had flown from his head. Hardly heard her answer, because he could observe the evidence for himself.

The baby boy had paled to parchment white, his skin textured like paper. On the monitor, his heart numbers had fallen, and they kept falling, while his blood pressure had climbed to dangerous heights. This had to be the aftermath of an IVH—an intraventricular haemorrhage.

A brain bleed, if you wanted to be totally blunt about it. Sometimes you didn't, because it sounded too scary, but the baby's parents weren't here right now, so there was no need to pretend.

The real problem was that the evidence only showed up, as now, after the event. You could treat the symptoms, but you couldn't prevent damage to the brain that might already have happened.

'So fast!' Carol said. 'He was at risk. They're always at risk, these ones—he's a twenty-eight-weeker, four days old—but he'd been looking so good and stable. Now…'

'I'm not calling Nguyen out of that conference,' Stephanie said.

Keelan cold-shouldered the technicality that this wasn't his domain.

'He needs something to boost his heart rate,' he said. 'And look at those sats.' He dredged his mind and found the weight-to-dosage figures he'd known by heart during his times in the NICU in the past, scaled down from the figures he usually needed upstairs but not so very different in principle.

He announced the result out loud, then added, 'That right, Stephanie? Carol?' They'd both nursed in this unit for years. They'd know if he'd somehow got it wrong, although he was sure he hadn't. Double-checking in his head, he saw both nurses nod.

Jessie also agreed. 'Yes, that's right.' Then she added, 'But let me tell Dr Richler what's going on.'

'You should,' Keelan said. 'I'm not waiting for her, though.'

This could have been Tam.

In the few seconds it had taken Keelan to react Carol had already begun to prepare the minuscule doses of medication while Stephanie had grabbed the equipment they'd need to bag oxygen into the baby boy in order to get those saturation figures on the monitor back up. Keelan snatched the bagging equipment from her and began to work on the baby. If he responded quickly to the treatment, they could cross their fingers that the bleed had been mild, no long-term effects, a small piece of bad luck instead of a terrible tragedy.

Because this could so easily have been Tam during his first days of life.

Jessie disappeared from Keelan's field of vision, her walk calm and steady and graceful as always. He forgot about her in the urgency of getting this baby right again, absolutely determined that one set of parents, at least, would be spared his own anguish today.

Lord, this blue-white, papery little face was so tiny and crumpled! He'd forgotten just how much delicacy of movement you needed. He held the bag in place, squeezed, counted, squeezed.

Come on, baby! Do this for me. For us. For your mum and dad. For *my* boy, Tam.

'Yep,' Carol said a few minutes later. 'Look. Sats are climbing. Colour's getting better.'

Ethan's blood pressure had fallen to a safer level, too, and his heart rate had improved. Another ten minutes and he had fully stabilised. You never would have known the bleed had happened, looking at his stats. They couldn't know for certain about the long-term consequences, but the outlook was promising, the way he'd bounced back so quickly.

Stepping back, letting go, Keelan found Cathy Richler standing there, the corner of her mouth quirked.

'Branching out?' she drawled.

'Call it a refresher course.' The closest he planned to get to an apology. 'I did consider this specialty, you know. And I have graduates of yours—' infant graduates, he meant '—in my care.'

'OK, I won't tell anyone,' she said. She and Keelan had always respected each other. 'Particularly since you got the right result. How bad did it look?'

Carol answered for him, reeling off the rock-bottom figures Ethan had reached seconds before they'd begun treatment.

'Hmm,' Cathy said, then leaned close to the incubator and addressed the baby, face-to-face. 'Drama king! What are we going to tell Mum and Dad, hey? They've gone out to lunch together, and I was the one who made them do it. They're going to think it was all their fault for not being here, little guy, you know that, don't you?'

Yeah, Keelan knew how that felt!

He decided to stay on until Daniel had a moment for him. Jessie sat in the one chair beside Tam, but when she saw the way he hovered, she stood up and said quietly, 'Can I get you something, Keelan? Coffee and a sandwich?'

'Mmm, please. That'd be nice,' he answered, feeling the usual wash of tenderness and magnetism that flowed between them.

That was what made it so hard. Magnetism…physical, chemical attraction…was one thing. You could box that up, keep it in its place, act cynical and call it raging animal libido. But when it came pre-blended with an equal mix of tenderness, the whole thing got a lot harder. Blame the babies, who made both him and Jessie feel like parents.

'Ham and salad?'

'Whatever comes.' His stomach felt hollow, but the hunger seemed distant and unimportant. He honestly didn't care. Cared far more about the look in her blue eyes, the little frown, the soft, concerned mouth. 'Just whatever,' he finished, the words like a reluctant hand pushing her away.

Daniel showed up before Jessie got back, and obviously knew from Keelan's face what he wanted to talk about. 'You want to take another look at the issue of surgery?'

'This isn't working, Daniel. It was for a while, when we were getting him over the infections, but now it's just the heart and we're going—he's going—one step forward and another step back. I'm not seeing what we're going to achieve here. He's so tired. He needs more help. Even with the risk.'

'Have you seen Keith? Said any of this to him?'

Keith Bedford was the paediatric heart surgeon who, with a junior surgeon assisting, would perform the operation to close the holes in Tam's tiny heart. Keelan knew him well, because he had paediatric heart patients of his own upstairs.

'No,' he answered. 'I wouldn't skirt your involvement on that. Let's present a united front. He's not going to be very keen.'

'Would you be?'

'I'd rather—I couldn't stand just watching him slide and slide, a little each day.'

'So is this about you? What you can stand?'

'No, it's about what Tam can stand. And I think he'd stand an aggressive boost, even with the risks, better than he's standing this wait-and-see, growing and feeding routine. It isn't working. I want to conclude that now, not wait to conclude it when it's definitively too late to act. And the harder the heart has to work, the more I'm concerned about the ticking time bomb of that thinned aorta wall. He needs the surgery.'

'Let's schedule a meeting with Keith. You want to be there?'

'Yes. Make it today, if we can. I can rejig most of my schedule, make the time. If we agree on this, Keith can operate Monday. I'm getting the worst feeling about waiting longer. And that's as a doctor, not a parent.' He stopped and frowned, heard the uncertainty vibrating in his own voice. 'Lord, I *think* that's as a doctor. Who the hell knows any more?'

He felt a soft touch on his sleeve. Jessie. With his sandwich and his coffee. She'd obviously heard enough of what he and Daniel had said to be able to put together the whole conversation. She looked very worried.

About him or about Tam?

Suddenly, he wanted her at the meeting with Keith and Daniel as well. For support. Input, even.

But then he braked hard on his emotions and got his perspective back. She had to get back to Tavie. She wasn't Tam's mother, or even officially—yet—his nurse. She didn't need to be there, and it wouldn't be fair to give her any responsibility for the decision.

He took the sandwich in its white paper bag and the coffee in its lidded styrofoam cup, and said, 'Thanks. Do you want to head off now?'

'Will you tell me when something's been decided? As soon as you can get to a phone?' She added quickly, 'Sorry, that's not fair of me, but I'm going to be thinking about it all afternoon.'

'It's fine. Of course I'll phone. It depends on Keith. I'm not sure of his schedule, when we'll be able to meet. And I'll try and get home for dinner, too.' It sounded like a promise from a busy husband to a neglected wife, but he didn't care.

She nodded, said goodbye to the nurses and Tam, and

left. He watched her go, and if Daniel and Stephanie and Carol were watching him watching her, and wondering why he couldn't drag his eyes away, he didn't care about that either.

At five-thirty, Jessie heard the rumble of the garage door when she'd just tiptoed into the baby's room to check that Tavie was still sleeping nicely. She'd been wakeful and fretful in the early afternoon, then she'd had a good feed and had settled down at around two. She would probably wake up again within the next half-hour.

At the familiar sound of Keelan's arrival home, Jessie felt a spurt of unreasonable anger—the channelling of a tension she'd been suffering under all afternoon.

Keelan had promised her that he'd phone as soon as he had any news, but she'd heard nothing, and she'd been on tenterhooks, wondering if the meeting had taken place. She couldn't imagine that Keelan would be home this early if he hadn't yet cornered Keith Bedford. He'd have waited at the hospital.

Entering the house, he saw her poised at the top of the stairs and said at once, 'I'm sorry, I know I told you I'd phone, but Keith and Daniel and I have only just finished our meeting. I didn't have anything else urgent, so it seemed best to come straight home and tell you in person.'

'Tell me…what?'

'He's willing to operate. He agrees that the real danger now is in waiting too long. Barring any unforeseen developments over the weekend, they'll do the surgery on Monday morning.'

'Whew!'

'You think that's the right decision?'

'Why are you asking me that, Keelan?' Jessie started down the stairs, as Keelan started up. 'I don't—'

'Because you said ''Whew'', as if you were relieved. As if you'd been waiting for this, and wanted it.'

'I— No, I mean, if you're relieved, then I'm relieved for you. I'm just…overwhelmed a bit. That's why the ''Whew''. It's—'

'Hey.' They reached each other in the middle of the stairs and stopped awkwardly. The treads were wide ones, but there wasn't a lot of room all the same. He brushed a strand of vibrant hair from her face. 'I'm treating it as good news. Don't fall apart on me.'

Jessie laughed, and it came out breathy and awkward. 'Sorry, is that not in my job description?'

'Most of this is not in your job description. None of this.'

The air vibrated, and Keelan put his hand on her arm to steady them both.

To keep that treacherous air in place.

Or something.

Jessie knew she ought not to look at his face. It wasn't safe. She couldn't help it, though. She wanted to—to drink in the painful pleasure of seeing him this close, feeling herself enveloped in his unique aura, sharing so much with him, watching his mouth when she was close enough to kiss it and his eyes when she could feel his gaze on her skin like radiant heat.

Every nerve ending in her body trembled and sang, and hot liquid seemed to pool inside her. The strength drained out of her legs like water from an open pipe. She really felt as if she couldn't stand and sank to the carpeted stairs, her fingers circled around his hard forearm, clinging to him for support.

She thought he'd follow her, sit beside her and consummate the touch of mouth to mouth that she could already taste, but he didn't, which left him towering over her, leaning a little because she still held onto his arm.

'You're just exhausted, aren't you?' he said.

'No. Yes. Of course.'

'Why didn't I see it?'

'Because you're exhausted, too.' She propped her elbow on her thigh and pillowed her cheek on the heel of her hand, waiting for something definitive to happen.

The kiss. Or the deliberate creation of distance.

Neither event did. Keelan and Jessie both simply stayed where they were on the stairs, clinging awkwardly to each other's arms. If he was looking at her the way she'd looked at him just now, she didn't know, because she'd at least managed to focus her eyes on the stair rails instead of his face.

'Listen, Mum wants us to bring Tavie up to see her,' he said finally. 'She told me when she was here that we'd both need a break within a few weeks, and she was right. We do.'

'But Tam's going into surgery on Monday.'

'Which means this weekend is our last chance until… Well, our last chance for a while.' He stopped, clearly fighting the spectre of possibilities that he didn't want to put into words, and that Jessie didn't even want to think about. If Tam didn't survive the surgery, they'd have plenty of chances to get away for a weekend in future.

'My schedule's pretty clear,' he went on after a moment. 'Tavie's strong enough to travel, if we're careful. Tam's in good care. Let's do it. I don't like the way you look today. Pale and wrung out and totally on edge. This weekend will be tough otherwise, hanging around waiting for the surgery on Monday. I don't think it'll do Tam any good at this stage to have us there, and these next weeks are going to be…'

Again, he stopped and didn't finish. They could only hope that the weeks ahead would be tiring, too, with all the time they'd be spending at the hospital, because if they weren't spending time at the hospital, it could only mean that the surgery on fragile Tam had failed.

'We could head up to Mum's late tomorrow afternoon,' Keelan continued. 'Take some snacks in the car and have a late meal when we get there. It's a great place, right on the beach, plenty of space and air. Bring a book and a swimsuit.'

Jessie laughed, somewhat shakily. 'You can stop, Keelan. I'm sold, OK? I'm packing. I'm digging out the swimsuit.'

He let her go at last and stepped carefully back down the stairs. 'It'll be good for both of us. I can work my schedule tomorrow so we can leave at four, if you can have Tavie ready.'

'If she co-operates.' Jessie hugged her arm against her chest, still feeling the sensation his touch had left on her skin. 'She was a bit fussy this afternoon, for a while. I didn't get much done until she finally fell asleep.'

'What would you like for dinner?' He stepped down another three treads, sliding his broad shoulders against the pale lemon-cream wall. 'Shall we eat late, take Tavie out for a stroll first, if she wakes up? It's a warm evening, and I think she's ready for another milestone.'

'A stroll would be great. Mica made a batch of pasta sauce yesterday. How does that sound?'

'Nice. With salad?'

He'd retreated all the way to the bottom of the stairs, and since both of them had just been gabbling at each other, with a tenth of their brains engaged, about the minutiae of their plans for the next two hours, the whole atmosphere felt safer now. Lighter. The air had stopped vibrating, and contained only the faint echo of all that awareness, like the echo that followed the dying sound of cathedral bells.

Jessie could breathe.

CHAPTER SEVEN

TAVIE took the journey to her grandmother's in stride like a veteran traveller…until the last twenty minutes of driving, when she suddenly decided that enough was enough and cried loudly for it to be over.

'She can't be hungry. Her nappy is fine. She's not sick.' Keelan ticked off the options for the fifth time.

'She's just frazzled,' Jessie said, also for the fifth time.

'And so are we.'

'Do you want to stop?' she asked.

They'd had a seductively pleasant drive until now. Hard to maintain any sort of distance when cocooned together in a moving car on a highway. It hadn't seemed particularly dangerous. They'd simply talked, or listened to music and news, or stayed silent.

But Jessie had no illusions. It wouldn't take much. The right touch or the right look at the wrong time, and the air would sing as if criss-crossed with firing bullets. Her heart would sing, too, no matter how much she tried not to hear it.

There had been an unspoken agreement that they weren't going to talk about Tam. Jessie had spent some time with him that morning, and they would see him again late Sunday afternoon when they returned to Sydney. Meanwhile, they knew he was in good hands, and they wanted this weekend to be about enjoying Tavie and getting a break.

By this time Jessie had grown used to the feeling of knowing where every bit of Keelan's body was positioned in relation to her own, of catching movements or gestures or voice tones from him that made her insides melt with wanting. She thought she could probably endure it, if she was careful, until it went away.

Which it would.

Surely.

It had with John Bishop, quite suddenly, after that telling argument about fidelity. She'd been left with regret and shame, but no longing or pain.

'What, you think we should set up camp by the side of the road?' Keelan said, in answer to her question about stopping, above the sound of Tavie's piercing cries. 'No, we have to get there, just get her peaceful and settled.'

They spilled noisily into Susan Hunter's spacious beach-front house some minutes later, bringing an atmosphere of chaos that Keelan's mother took cheerfully in her stride. 'And here's your Aunt Lynette, Keelan.' Another woman, clearly Susan's sister, hovered in the background. 'She's here to give me grandmother lessons, and I'm obviously going to need them.'

'I'm sorry, Mum. We think she's just stressed from the drive. She slept most of the way, until just this last…month, it feels like. Year.'

'Twenty minutes,' Jessie corrected, squeezing out a smile. 'We fed her halfway, and had a snack ourselves. I think we should try a bottle, Keelan, just to soothe her, even if she's not very hungry. Can I sit somewhere quiet with her?'

'Let me show you where I've put you all,' Susan said. 'There's an armchair in the baby's room.'

'I can make up her bottle,' Keelan's aunt offered.

'Here's her bag,' he said and tossed it to her like a rugby ball, without even looking to see if it had found its mark. His eyes were on crying Tavie again. 'The formula's in the tin, should be near the top. Don't overheat it.'

'If I could have a couple of pillows in the chair...' Jessie suggested.

'Four adults, one baby, and it still feels like we don't have enough pairs of hands,' Susan said.

But it broke the ice, and by the time Tavie finally settled, stopped crying and went to sleep, Jessie had forgotten that she didn't quite know how she fitted in here in Susan Hunter's lovely home, and whether she was viewed as a friend or an employee...or some other option she hadn't even considered, because she didn't dare to.

The house was gorgeous, with views, through its huge windows, over the dunes to the beach. On a wide wooden deck that looked silver in the moonlight, there was an awning for daytime shade, an outdoor table and chairs, and a big gas barbecue. Inside, the floors were tiled in cool ceramic or glowing polished cork, and the decor had a relaxed, summery feel, with lots of blue and white.

You could hear the ocean in the background, eternally washing and crashing onto the sand.

As well as Keelan's mother and aunt, Lynette's husband Alan was also there for the weekend. A keen fisherman, he warned everyone not to expect much in the way of baby-care from him, but possibly they'd get something nice and fresh from the ocean for breakfast. He'd be rising before dawn to try his luck on the rocky tidal shelf just to the south.

Keelan didn't attempt to persuade him to take more of an interest in his little adoptive great-niece. Tavie's immune system would still be fragile, so it didn't make sense to have too many people closely involved in her care.

Keelan and Jessie hadn't eaten yet, even though it was

now after nine, but the delectable aroma issuing from the kitchen suggested that dinner had been saved for them—a chicken and white wine casserole with mushrooms, sour cream, herbs and vegetables, served on a bed of fluffy rice.

After the delicious meal, Keelan's mother and aunt both pushed Jessie in the direction of an enormous bathtub in a palatial bathroom. Susan even lit candles and an aromatherapy oil burner, then produced a huge, fluffy blue towel and told her, 'Don't you dare fight this, because you're here for a break. I'm not having my granddaughter's primary carer collapse in an exhausted heap.'

She finished in a different tone, over the sound of hot water plunging into the porcelain tub, 'And Tam's going to need your strength and energy over the next few weeks. Keelan, too.' Another pause. 'Keelan, most of all.'

Tavie only woke up once during the night, and they'd already agreed that Keelan would go to her, so Jessie didn't even hear about it until breakfast. She'd slept wonderfully, and felt as cosseted as a pedigreed cat.

Keelan's aunt brought her a late breakfast of coffee, pink grapefruit, croissants and grilled tailor-fish that had still been swimming a couple of hours ago, with fresh bread, butter and lemon, and she ate it out on the deck. She couldn't remember ever being spoiled like this in her life.

'We have the day all planned out,' Lynette Schaeffer said. 'Morning here on the sun deck with the weekend newspapers, while Sue and I take the baby for a stroll. A simple lunch. Tavie has a big nap in the afternoon, after all the fresh air, and you and Keelan head for the beach. Tonight, we'll babysit, while he takes you to a wonderful Italian restaurant in Handley Head, overlooking the water.'

'Has Keelan signed off on this?' Jessie had to ask. 'Where is he?'

'He's in the shower. And he will sign off on it. His mother can be very persuasive! And when I tell her you've agreed...'

'But I haven't. Have I?'

'Your face is speaking for you. Don't fight it, dear.'

On the strength of this cryptic comment, Jessie wondered, with a fluttery stomach, just how much Susan had seen and guessed during her Sydney visit, and how much conspiring she and her sister had done.

I *am* fighting it, though, she thought. I have to...

But then, just a little while later, Tavie stepped in and joined the conspiracy, and at that point Jessie couldn't pretend to herself any longer about anything.

They had the baby girl all ready to go for her morning walk, as per the plan, lying on her sheepskin in the pram, swaddled in blankets, shaded by the canopy, protected with netting and recently fed. She still seemed tiny to her great-aunt Lynette, who was used to her own very robust grandchildren, but the way she kicked and looked so alert, no one could doubt that she was getting stronger every day.

And the two older women, Keelan and Jessie were all grouped around the pram, down on the path that ran in front of the house, when Tavie reached a milestone they'd all been talking about and waiting for, but hadn't yet seen.

She smiled.

'At me!' Jessie said, emotion flooding her in a painful rush. 'Oh, you're smiling at me!'

Tavie didn't just smile with her mouth and her eyes

when she saw that familiar human shape bending over her. She seemed to smile with every muscle in her body. Her little hands stretched like pink starfish, her breathing went fast and excited, and her whole face lit up.

'Oh, let's see!' Susan said. 'Keep doing it for Grandma, darling. Grandma wants to see, too.'

Tavie obliged. Her dad got one, and even her great-aunt. But the best and longest smile came when she looked at Jessie.

How can I ever let this go? Jessie wondered, her stomach rolling at the thought of what she'd lose when Keelan didn't need her any more, just a couple of months from now. She'd lose far more than she could put into words, far more than she even dared to think about. The baby, the man, a home that was warmer and better than anything she'd ever imagined.

She wouldn't think about it. She couldn't afford to…

The realisation came anyway, despite the desperate fire wall she'd tried to construct inside her head.

She'd fallen in love with Keelan, and all her barriers lay in ruins.

When? How?

She could try to map it all out, pinpoint each subtle or sudden change in her perceptions, but even if she succeeded, it wouldn't change the basic fact, she knew. Love didn't operate that way.

Suddenly one day it was just there, as much a part of you as, say, your taste for spicy food or your aversion to the smell of mint toothpaste. And it could feel as frightening inside you as a newly diagnosed disease or an unexpected stab of pain.

Beside her, standing close, Keelan laughed. 'Wow! Oh, wow!'

He sounded choky and tight in the throat, as if he

couldn't risk more words without breaking down. Jessie wanted to reach out for him, hug him and hold him and lean on him while they watched the baby together, but this wasn't her right, or her role, and that felt more frightening than ever, now that she understood what had happened inside her.

How can I let any of this go? she thought. It's going to tear out my heart.

A minute later, Susan and Lynette set off with the pram, leaving Keelan and Jessie free.

And alone.

Neither of them was used to it. In Sydney, they always had something or someone to hide behind. Keelan's work. Mica Sagovic's cheerful, slightly bossy presence. Tavie. Now they both stepped back from each other instinctively, as if they needed greater distance now that their three chaperones were gone. Keelan's uncle had also gone out—to the local bait shop to discuss tides and other fishing-related topics.

'We're supposed to read the paper now, I think,' Jessie murmured. She still felt shaky inside, dizzy and sick and hugely off-balance, as if she'd been tumbled over and over through the water by a rogue wave.

'On the deck,' Keelan agreed. 'Sipping cool drinks when the sun gets hotter.'

She manufactured a laugh. 'Oh, you got the bulletin, too?'

'I did.' He shrugged, and gave that delicious smile of his, suggesting its usual shared secret.

They turned and began to walk back towards the house, still keeping carefully apart.

'I wonder,' Jessie said, speaking too fast, 'if you could ask your mother and your aunt to stop treating me like family.'

And you and me like a couple.

'Is that what they're doing?' Keelan opened the door for her, and let her precede him up the stairs that opened beyond the entranceway. Passing him, her skin tingled and she couldn't breathe. 'They claim they're only treating you like a friend who needs a break.'

'But you don't buy that either, do you?' Still a little breathless, she flung the question over her shoulder on her way up the stairs.

'Not entirely.'

'So you've talked to them about it already.'

He shrugged, skirted around her and picked the weekend newspapers off the coffee-table. 'I had a word or two.'

'When?'

'Last night.'

'Well, then, it hasn't done any good, because they're still doing it this morning.'

And I like it too much. I'm greedy for everything I want it to mean.

'We can ride it out,' he said calmly, as if it didn't matter much. 'It's only until tomorrow. Here, have the *Herald.*' He handed her the thick fold of newsprint, but their fingers didn't touch. 'I'll take the *Australian.* We can ignore each other all morning, if you want.'

'I don't want—I'm not avoiding you. I just don't want—'

'Them thinking what they're thinking?' His voice dropped. 'About us?'

He'd come right out and said it.

'Yes,' Jessie answered. 'That.'

She hugged the paper to her chest like a shield, and they stared at each other, all pretence dropping away. An electric charge filled the air, softening every bone in her body. Keelan put the second newspaper back on the coffee-table in an untidy heap and stepped towards her. He was close enough to touch her, but he didn't. The possibility that he soon would seemed like both a promise and a threat.

'What exactly is it that's stopping us from acting on this, Jessie?' he said. 'Remind me. Because I'm not sure that I know the reason any more. I did know, but it's been swamped by…other things. Left behind in Sydney, or something. I kept thinking this would go away, that we could push it away by avoiding each other, but it hasn't gone at all.'

'Yet,' she insisted, hugging the newspaper tighter against her body.

'So you still think it will?'

'Oh, yes!'

For him, if not for her.

'You're quite a cynic, aren't you?' His eyes dropped to her mouth, as if to suggest that she told sweet lies from time to time as well.

Was she a cynic? she wondered.

In regard to John, yes, but only because of how badly he'd hurt her, how unscathed he'd been at the end of it in contrast, and how much she regretted her own decisions. In too many other areas of her life she wasn't nearly cynical enough. She only pretended.

Her heart was a puppy asleep in front of a tractor wheel, completely vulnerable unless it woke up in time.

One whole, huge, naïve part of her desperately didn't want this feeling for Keelan to *ever* go away. It felt too good and too important—nourishing her, making her dizzy, giving her hope and home, and terrifying her, all at the same time.

The rest of her winced and shuddered, waiting to get

crushed, and she didn't want him to know anything about how she really felt.

The depth of it. The strength of it.

'I suppose I am…somewhat cynical in some areas,' she answered him coolly, because this answer seemed safest.

'So tell me why we shouldn't just go with it, give in to it, enjoy it,' Keelan said.

His brown eyes raked over her again, touching on her lips, which she scraped nervously with her teeth, and her wrists, bent across the newspaper.

'Cynicism is an asset in a situation like this, isn't it?' he went on, and his voice had the texture of raw silk. 'Plenty of people launch into relationships they know have zero likelihood of lasting, and surely that's part of the appeal.'

'Zero likelihood…' She gave a cautious little laugh. 'Yes. My track record isn't good, is it? Personally or professionally. If it was, I wouldn't be here in the first place. I'd still be…somewhere else.'

Adelaide. She'd had a relationship there that hadn't lasted. London. Or somewhere in the developing world with the doctor who'd been her lover in Sierra Leone and who was still, judging from the occasional postcard, totally wedded to his work. She couldn't even remember, now, how she'd felt about him.

Nothing like this.

Nothing anywhere near as dangerous and turbulent as this.

'Plenty of people see that as a plus,' Keelan was saying. 'The fact that it has to be short term. And it seems as if you're one of them, so present your case.'

'I have no case to present. I'm not sure what you're saying, Keelan, or what you want.'

'Oh, you know what I want.' He moved closer, his open hands hovering lightly near her elbows, which were angled outwards because of the wad of newsprint she still clutched against her chest.

'Sex,' she suggested bluntly, because the word was practically written across his face in big block capitals.

'For starters,' he agreed, just as bluntly. 'To be honest, you've got me so close to the brink I'm not going to be able to think straight until we get that out of the way. If we do.'

Their eyes met once again, and she knew that he could have left off those last three words. They weren't necessary. They didn't apply. There was no 'if' any more. Sometime between driving up from Sydney last night and standing here with Keelan right now, 'if' had evaporated completely. Now there was only 'when'.

'Let's talk about it,' he suggested, his voice dropping to a growl. 'You've sampled different professional environments on several continents. Big, richly endowed hospitals, tiny, primitive clinics, attractive private homes. I'm not going to assume that you've sampled relationships in the same way, but...have you?'

'A couple of times.' What did she want him to think? What would protect her best? 'Yes, several times.'

'With no intention of looking for something that might last? You have no desire for that?'

'Sometimes things do last,' she said. 'But I'm a realist. Haven't we talked about this? I'm sure you'd only get serious about a woman who has a lot more to offer than I do.'

'Hell, do you doubt yourself that much?'

'I don't doubt myself.' She lifted her chin instinctively. 'But I do have a healthy awareness of our differences. You're not going to risk messing up your life with a relationship that doesn't fit the mould. You're not going to risk squandering your assets.'

'My assets?'

'Your family, your background, your reputation, your rock-solid position in every area of your life.' She spoke as dispassionately as she could, wondering if he would argue. 'The assets you want for the twins, too. You'll want a capital gain when you marry, an advantageous alliance, someone you're sure of on paper, as well as someone you love.'

'I've been married before, you know.'

'Yes, you've mentioned it. Tanya.' She said the name with a deliberate sourness, even though she felt no genuine hostility towards Keelan's ex-wife. 'And wasn't she a doctor? From a very well-established New Zealand family?'

'Yes, she was. And it didn't last. I've been thinking about that lately.'

'And you've concluded that this time around you're looking for a serious commitment with a lower middle-class, footloose nurse, with a fractured, uncaring family and a dubious sexual history on three continents? I don't think so!'

He pivoted on his heel and made a sound deep in his throat that she couldn't interpret. 'Don't put yourself down! Don't you think you're insulting both of us with that statement?'

No, I'm just putting some essential protection in place before I give in, trying to find out where you stand. Being realistic.

'If we're going to do this, let's shatter the illusions before, not after, Keelan,' she said coolly, burning up inside.

'Right. Go ahead. Shatter away. Because we're definitely doing this.' He stepped close again, and laced his arms loosely around her. She felt the power of her body's response, like water dragging on a rudderless boat in a strong current. 'And soon.'

'It's an affair,' she said, giving him what he wanted. 'It's not going to last.' Time for greater honesty now. 'It's going to hurt at the end...'

'Yeah?'

'I already know that. And it's...nothing to do with you in a way. Part of it. It's because of the way Tavie smiled at me just now. I—I couldn't care *for* her without caring *about* her, and she's not mine, so—'

'No reason you can't stay in her life, is there, even if you don't meaningfully stay in mine? Get a hospital job in Sydney, and visit her whenever you want. Tam, too. Be their Auntie Jessie.'

Jessie closed her eyes and shook her head. 'I'm not staying in Sydney.' She looked into his face again. 'I'll take another assignment with Médecins Sans Frontières probably.'

Again, she said it in as cool and practical a tone as she could, making it sound like a positive plan instead of a blind escape and a desperate bid to get her priorities back. She couldn't stay in Sydney purely in order to fill a peripheral role in another family's life, once Keelan's inappropriate, inconvenient attraction to her had flared and burned out.

Now, feeling as she did, she knew there had to be more. If she gave herself to this, was she opening a tiny chink of hope that one day there might be, or was she sabotaging that hope forever?

'What about hurting me?' Keelan asked lightly. 'Any predictions on that?'

'Men can get hurt, too. Of course. I think there'll be

some regret. Of course,' she repeated ineptly. Her voice didn't come out nearly as cool as she wanted it to. 'Endings are often messy, and while some men don't mind mess in their living space, most run a mile from it in their emotional lives. They want everything clean and uncluttered. My prediction? You'll be thoroughly glad if I get on a plane and fly far, far away. Like Tanya did.'

'You don't think you'll break my heart?'

'No. I don't. You're too sensible for that. Too much else on your plate. And too much in control.'

He had to be in control, because she certainly wasn't.

They stared at each other again.

'OK,' he said, after a moment. 'You've shattered the illusions. Now I'll set out the ground rules.'

'I guess there would have to be a few of those.'

'This ends when you leave—and when you leave is a decision either of us can make. But while it's happening, it's not half-hearted. It's exclusive. Nothing on the side. It's intense. Sexually, and in every other way. It's not something we hide, and it's not something we flaunt. It just is.'

'Those aren't quite the rules I expected.'

'No?'

She shrugged, aware that she'd flushed a little. She felt the slide of his hands across her skin.

'I thought there might be more about boundaries,' she said. 'No waking up in the same bed or something. And discretion. Not letting anyone get the wrong idea. Never getting seen at certain restaurants.'

'Nope, there's none of that. Are you ever going to put down that newspaper? I think it's safe now.'

Jessie laughed, and blurted out the most honest statement she'd made in minutes. 'There's nothing safe about this.'

'No,' he said slowly. He pried her arms loose and took the newspaper. Looking down, she saw that the ink had left black smears on her pale blue top, darkest where the print had pressed against her breasts. 'That's one thing we might both agree on without further negotiation. Seems like part of the attraction. That we're heading into the danger of the unknown.'

Right now.

Right at the moment when his mouth touched hers.

The newspaper rustled as it dropped onto the table, and Jessie didn't give it another thought. The first time Keelan had kissed her, it had been blind, rather desperate, full of an uncertainty that had come from both of them. This time it was intensely sensual—no, *sexual*, why beat around the bush?—and both of them knew that they weren't willingly turning back.

Keelan held Jessie's shoulders and printed her lips with the heat of his mouth, like some potent, fiery liquor. Her whole being seemed to arrow into this one seamless, endless point of contact. Every sense channelled into it, like a high tide funnelling into a deep, narrow strait. And every emotion channelled into it, too—the love she'd discovered, the passionate need to stay in his life, to mother his babies and to belong. All of this, in one kiss.

Gradually, however, their bodies shifted closer, fitting together like a hand sliding into a glove. Her breasts against his chest, her hips against his groin, two pairs of thighs like jointed woodwork.

His arms wrapped around her, cradling most of her weight. She felt as boneless as a piece of fabric, her body held together only by the beating of the blood through her veins.

'Keelan…' His name made a sigh in her mouth.

She sounded as if she was begging for the next step,

and this was the meaning he took from that one breathless word. 'Yes,' he said. 'We'll go to my room.'

She didn't argue, didn't even want to.

They moved as far as the corridor, pulling on each other's arms, but then he groaned and stopped, pressed her shoulder blades up against the wall and pulled her hips roughly towards him with both hands. She arched her back, gasped and swallowed and kissed him fiercely again, wanting him to feel the way her nipples jutted, and to understand the pleasure she felt when she kneaded the muscles of his back with her fingers.

Impatient and clumsy, she dragged his sage-green polo shirt up to his armpits, until he completed the action for her, reaching around to pull it forward over his head. He tossed it through the open doorway of his room, and then she ran the palms of her hands down his chest, exulting in the hard, hair-roughened planes she'd known she would find.

In this moment, those planes of skin and muscle belonged only to her, and she explored them in naked appreciation of her new right of possession.

'Take your top off, too,' he told her.

His words were rough and careless, and he didn't try to disguise the way he kept his eyes on her body, waiting for what he'd see next. His open need aroused her even further, made her pulse and crumble inside.

Every inch of skin on fire, she complied with what he'd asked, crossing her arms, taking the fabric in her grip and pulling it upward. She heard rather than saw the moment when he caught sight of her breasts, cupped in a dark blue lace bra. His breath hissed across his teeth and shuddered into his lungs.

Above her head, the top tangled around her wrists,

handcuffing her arms back against the wall and jutting her upper body forward.

Keelan took full advantage of her temporary imprisonment. He splayed his hands over her stretched ribs and buried his face in the valley between her breasts. Her torso twisted with pleasure and he slid his hands higher, cupping the lace and thumbing the edge of the fabric down to release her nipple into his waiting mouth.

She writhed and flapped ineffectually at the twisted top, didn't much care if she had to stay like this a bit longer. Be honest, she could have freed herself if she'd wanted to. She wondered if she'd ever want to, but couldn't imagine it right now.

Keelan slid his hands inside the back waistband of her jeans and traced the taut contours of her cheeks beyond the high-cut edge of her underwear, and the sensitive crease where thighs and bottom joined. He kissed her mouth and her neck, then came back to her breasts and ravaged them, making them swell and ache.

'I'm stuck in this top,' she breathed. 'Let me get free, because I want to—'

Women's voices sounded outside, and Keelan suddenly stilled at the same moment that Jessie's unfinished sentence cut out. They both listened, and recognised his mother and his aunt, locked in chatty, sisterly talk, as well as something about Tavie's nappy-change bag.

They hadn't brought it with them, but should have done. They didn't want to disrupt Keelan's and Jessie's tranquil morning, but it couldn't be helped.

The doorknob downstairs rattled a little as it opened.

Keelan didn't say a word at first. Eyes fixed on Jessie's face, he nudged his thigh between her legs to press into the swollen heat that pulsed against the centre seam of her jeans. Then he gave her one last, searing kiss, eased back and lifted his arm to lower her hands and twisted sleeves down in front of her.

'Later,' he finally muttered. 'I guess this has to happen later.'

'Yes,' she agreed, not knowing how either of them would stand the wait.

CHAPTER EIGHT

THE cold salt water felt fabulous on Jessie's over-heated body. She wore a navy and white tank-style swimsuit that seemed to cling far too closely and reveal far too much today, although by any Australian standard it wasn't a provocative garment.

There were only a few other swimmers on the beach, since the water in November still contained the chill of winter. Beside her Keelan body-surfed, launching himself forward in the curve of each wave just before it broke and powering towards the shore amidst the tumbling white foam.

Lunch had seemed like one long ache of awareness between the two of them. A couple of times Jessie could have sworn she'd seen a significant, satisfied look pass between Susan and her sister. But then she had come to her senses and realised that they'd just been smiling at Tavie, fast asleep in her canopied pram between the two older women, knocked out by the fresh sea air just as Keelan's aunt had predicted she would be.

There had been no earth-shattering understanding passing between the two sisters in regard to what had happened between Keelan and herself. Jessie was the only person in Tavie's life whose world had completely shifted on its axis today.

'Off to the beach, you two,' Lynette ordered, a little later. 'It's getting quite hot. We'll feed her if she wakes up.'

'The bottle is—'

'I know all about bottles, Jessie, don't worry.'

So here they were, herself and Keelan, pretending that all they could think about was the water, the sun and the salt, when really…

Oh, dear heaven, Keelan's body was gorgeous!

Jessie had taken this in from day one as a simple fact. His whole frame was so strong and so confident and so beautifully built. Any woman with breath in her body would have to see it. Now her awareness of him was very different, however. So much more personal, so much more detailed, and filled with a hunger and a need that she didn't know how she'd ever assuage, no matter how heated and intense their affair became.

They had claimed ownership of each other this morning, and that had seemed so right and inevitable and necessary, but now she felt a little frightened again, wondering if it might be possible to put on the brakes, wondering if she should want to.

There was a term for it in the area of commerce, she thought—the cooling-off period. Some kind of contractual window during which the buyer could change his or her mind and not make the purchase after all.

Tavie's urgent need for a nappy change this morning had given Jessie and Keelan a cooling-off period. They needn't go through with this after all. They could cool their heated libidos and renege on the entire agreement.

But, no, she didn't want to renege, or to cool anything.

She wanted Keelan more than ever, her senses pushed to the brink by what had happened between them this morning, and by what had happened so powerfully in her heart. The sea might be cooling her skin, but it couldn't cool her feelings. Every time he looked at her, she got that helpless, boneless, light-headed feeling again, and it both exulted and terrified her.

So this was what love felt like.

'Had enough?' he asked finally, as they stood in the shallows with the foam still churning around their legs. Water glistened and streamed on his chest and arms, and down his thighs below the baggy black board-shorts he wore. 'Your lips are going blue, and my ears are aching.'

'It's great,' she answered breathlessly. 'But, yes, I've had enough.'

'Next on the agenda, we're supposed to go for a walk.'

'Right.'

'But we can stage a revolution, if you want, and refuse to submit to this dictatorial conspiracy.'

'I'm OK with a walk,' she drawled, through closed lips.

'Beach to the north is pretty deserted, especially once you get to the headland.'

'So are you saying you want to head south?'

'No. I'm not.' His eyes were fixed on her face, and filled with a light that Jessie couldn't misinterpret or ignore. 'I'm voting for north.'

She couldn't find words or breath to answer.

They left the water, found their towels and buffed the salt water from their bodies. Keelan put on his polo shirt and Jessie slipped into her strappy lemon yellow sundress, still without speaking. At first they walked just where the highest-reaching waves sank their frilly edges into the sand, but Jessie had had enough of the cold water and soon moved to where the sand was dry.

'Still chilly?' Keelan asked her, and her nod gave him the cue they'd both been looking for.

He put his arm around her and pulled her close against his side. She laid her head on his shoulder, and felt his mouth press her temple and her hair, both places sticky with drying salt.

'You're very quiet,' he said after a moment.

She laughed, knowing he wouldn't understand her odd, upside-down source of amusement. 'Nothing to say.'

Everything to say.

That would have been more truthful, and that was why she had laughed.

She simply didn't dare to open her mouth, for fear of what might spill out—foolish words of love that she knew he would never say in return, feverish demands for a reassurance that he would never give.

Perhaps he'd been right earlier.

She did doubt herself.

Or she doubted her place in the universe. Why should *she* be blessed with something miraculous and right and lasting, when so many people got it wrong, and when she'd got it so disastrously wrong herself, with John Bishop, in similar circumstances? Whatever the magic ingredient was that allowed someone to find that kind of love, she wasn't at all convinced that she had it, or knew it.

'Silence is nice,' Keelan said.

'Mmm.'

Because I can put all my energy into remembering to breathe, she added inwardly.

'I won't ask what you're thinking, but I'll tell you what I'm thinking,' he offered.

'Yes?'

'Wondering just how secluded it is…in the lee of that headland. If there's no one there, and if there's a sheltered patch of grass…'

'It's not that secluded!'

He laughed this time. 'Putting me and my male needs firmly in place?'

She took a steadying breath and confessed, 'And mine. My needs are just as— But I'm being…practical.'

Cool-headed.

As far as that was possible.

'I guess sand is not an ingredient we really want this time around,' he conceded. He brushed some grains of the stuff from her forearm as he spoke.

'Other times, though?' She smiled, turned to him and did the same, where some adhered to his jaw. 'Have to admit, it hasn't ever entered my fantasies.'

'Next time we'll bring our towels. And you can tell me a bit more about those fantasies of yours. Show me a couple.'

Her fantasies? There was really only one, at this moment—the fantasy that, strong as it was, this shared desire for each other was just one part of a complete package.

Jessie closed her mouth firmly again and pressed her lips tightly against her teeth, to make sure she didn't say it.

They kissed, of course, in the secluded lee of the headland Keelan had talked about. Waiting for it, she could have thrown herself against his chest and begged, but managed to retain enough control to spare them both such an embarrassing degree of emotion.

Instead, he was the one who took the initiative.

'The breeze has dropped here,' he said. 'We're protected by the cliff. You feel much warmer now.' He ran his hand lightly down her arm. 'Delicious. Radiating heat.'

'So do you,' she managed to answer, as he turned her in his arms.

His skin had been buffed by the wind and the waves, and felt as smooth as polished stone baked in the sun.

She slid her hands up inside his shirt at once, splaying her fingers across his back.

'Your mouth has turned pink again.' He touched it lightly with his lips, just a soft brushstroke of sensation. 'And you taste…warm, salty.'

'So do you,' she repeated.

She closed her eyes as he tasted her again, his mouth still soft and light on hers. She had to fight to hold herself back to his lazy, leisurely pace, and it made her ache in impossible places. He wasn't planning to rush this, to go too deep, too soon, yet she was already trembling.

A sound of need escaped from her throat like a bubble rising in water, and she would have whimpered if she hadn't dammed the feeling back. Was this really as easy for him as it seemed?

No, perhaps it wasn't.

His control suddenly seemed to break, and their kiss deepened the way a flowing stream could suddenly deepen into a dark, spinning pool. His arms tightened around her, the bruising press of his mouth parted her lips and drew her tongue into a sinuous dance. She lifted her hand to the back of his head and ran her fingers up through his hair, loving the shape and the texture and the scents of sea water and shampoo that she released into the air.

'You're fabulous…beautiful,' he said raggedly. 'I want you right now, and the only way, let me tell you, that I'm going to stand the wait is by promising both of us that it will be even better that way. If we've held back just a little. If we've had to dam this inside us. It will be…better…even better than what we have now.'

'Yes. Oh, yes.'

Sliding her dress up her thighs, he cupped her bottom through the still-damp fabric of her swimsuit, and Jessie felt the weight and heat of his arousal hard and insistent against her.

Yes. She had this, at least. This proof of need and connection.

With a shock, she realised she'd never wanted a man quite this nakedly, this physically. Giving herself to John, she'd surrounded herself with a misty glow of romance and sacrifice. Only in hindsight had she acknowledged that their love-making had often been a disappointment to her on a sensual level. A few years earlier, when she had assuaged the fatigue and stress of work in an African clinic with Gary, they had both been looking for time out and release more than a truly passionate connection.

This felt different.

This felt like something she should run a hundred miles to avoid because it might so easily shatter her into pieces, only she didn't have the will or the strength to run anywhere. Instead, she shored her weakened limbs more firmly against Keelan and gave him everything she had with her kiss.

By the time they stopped, both were breathless and dishevelled. Jessie's dress and swimsuit straps had slipped down her arms until the tops of her breasts threatened to spill into Keelan's demanding hands, or his even more demanding mouth. Her hair, already tangled by the sea, whipped across her face in salty strands so that he had to push it aside with impatient fingers to keep his delectable contact with her lips.

When his hold on her finally eased, she felt the shuddering breath he drew and heard the edge in his laugh.

'I'm starting to repeat blatant lies to myself about sand,' he said, mocking himself. 'And beachcombers. Wouldn't be so bad, would it? If our skin got chafed? If someone wandered past? With a camera? And no one's going to, are they?'

'Keelan—'

'Don't worry. Not serious here. Very serious, but not about here. Later. We're going to dinner, and—'

'Yes, dinner's in the plan. But there's nothing mentioned about after dinner.' Jessie didn't know if she was teasing him or what. Looking into his brown eyes, she saw the suffering, and the amusement, and wondered what her own expression said back to him. More of the same, she guessed.

'Dinner's an ambiguous word,' he answered, 'and it fills an open-ended slot. I could feast on you. Cover you in whipped cream and lick it off. Or put a chocolate-coated strawberry between our lips and—'

'Mmm!' She closed her eyes, almost tasting the sweet red juice of the fruit, mingled with the taste of him.

'That would be dinner,' he claimed. 'Dessert. Definitely in the plan.'

Weakly, she leaned her forehead into his shoulder and told him, 'I'm not going to argue this with you on the basis of what the word ''dinner'' means.'

'But you're going to argue?'

'Maybe. I don't think so. I don't know.'

'Have to warn you, I'm going to take that as a challenge. By the end of the evening, you'll know.'

'Hello?' Keelan murmured, as they came along the path between the dunes half an hour later and arrived within sight of the house. 'There's another car out the—' He stopped and swore. 'That's Dad!'

Jessie sensed his immediate wariness, although they weren't touching. She could almost hear the questions jangling inside his head as well. After a moment of strained silence, he began to speak them out loud, answering most of them himself in the same breath.

'What's he doing here? Did Mum know he was coming, I wonder? Can't imagine she did. What's the time? Must be well after four. I should have worn my watch. He's not planning to stay, surely?'

Jessie listened to the litany until this last question, then cut in with one of her own. 'He knew we were coming up?'

'Yes, I mentioned it to him Thursday evening when he phoned.'

Since Dawson Hunter's first two visits to Tavie, he'd begun to drop in a couple of times a week to spend time with his granddaughter, and he expected regular reports from his son by phone as well.

Keelan didn't say anything more, and they reached the house a minute later. Upstairs on the sun deck, they realised that Dawson must have only just arrived.

The atmosphere seemed strained, though he looked relieved to see his son, as if counting on him as an ally. Alan offered his ex-brother-in-law a beer, but apparently no one heard. Dawson himself said in a tone of mingled defensiveness and belligerence, 'I knew this would be a big weekend for her, and I wanted to see for myself how she was doing. I dropped in. Is that wrong, Susan?'

'Dropped in? It's a four-hour drive.'

'Hmm. I can do it in three and a half, if the traffic cooperates,' he muttered. 'Send me straight back, if you feel so strongly about it.'

'I—I don't.' Susan spread her hands. 'Not really. I just wish you'd—'

'Warned you?'

'Yes, if I'm honest!'

'So you could, what?'

'Make up a bed for you in the laundry alcove downstairs, because that's about all the room we've got left.'

'And that's where you'd put a visiting dog.'

'Dawson…'

'Dad,' Keelan said, stepping into the fray. 'Specialist in knocking us all for a loop.' He clapped his father on the back. 'Tavie's doing really well, if you were worried.'

'Of course I was. She's so small for a long car journey.'

'She got a bit frazzled by the end, but she settled down as soon as we got her into a quiet environment and gave her a feed. She's been great today, hasn't she, Mum?'

'She had a bottle at three, but now she's back asleep, like a little lamb,' his mother confirmed.

'Beer, Dawson?' Alan repeated, and this time he got a grateful nod.

Lynette and Susan exchanged significant looks, and this time Jessie knew her imagination wasn't playing tricks when she read their meaning.

Lynette's look said, Why don't you just kick him out right now?

Susan's answered, Because I have a horrible feeling I don't want to, even though I probably should.

Next, after a strained pause, Lynette announced aloud, 'Alan and I were thinking of going to the club for dinner tonight, by the way, Susan, as long as you're feeling comfortable with Tavie.'

'Club?' Alan queried, not quick enough on the uptake to please his wife. 'What club?'

'Any club, Alan, for heaven's sake! The RSL, the Surf Lifesavers, the golf club. Wherever we like.'

'I thought we were— Oh. Yes. Give other people a quiet night, if they want one.' He telegraphed a hunted look towards Susan and Dawson that told everyone he'd got the point now. Leave the two of them alone to sort something out, whether they wanted to or not. 'Of course. That was the plan, wasn't it? You're going out, too, aren't you, Keelan? Jessie?'

'Yes, but they're not going to the club,' Lynette answered for them, in a tone decisive enough to sharpen a blunt axe. 'They're going to that lovely Italian place, just the two of them. Early. So they can start with a relaxed drink at the bar. And that's what we're doing, too. And since it's almost five, those of us who are showering had better start.'

'That's me,' Keelan said.

'And me,' Jessie added. There were two bathrooms.

'We don't need to, do we, Alan?' Lynette decided. 'I'll change—it'll take thirty seconds—and then we can head off. Phone me on my mobile, Sue, if you need me home again.'

'I…uh…' Keelan's mother trailed off, looking helplessly at her ex-husband, her pushy sister, her unhelpful son. 'I imagine Dawson and I will be able to manage between us.'

'Her two grandparents,' Dawson said, then turned to his ex-wife. 'Susie? Will you give it a try?'

It was so painfully apparent that he was asking about far more than just a single evening of shared babysitting that every molecule of air in the room suddenly seemed as fragile as spun glass. Jessie held her breath, unbearably moved by the naked, vulnerable appeal in such a large, arrogant and successful man, and by the emotion and uncertainty that Susan showed.

She couldn't answer her ex-husband at first. Her hands worked and twisted in front of her, and her mouth fell open, though no sound came out.

'I need…a lot of time,' she finally said in a strangled voice. 'I need…a lot more than this.'

'But it's a start, Susie,' came Dawson's hoarse voice. Jessie had already begun her retreat into the house, with Keelan, Lynette and Alan close behind her. 'Just tell me it might be a start.'

If Susan answered, it wasn't audible from this distance.

'How would you feel about it, Keelan, if they did get back together?' Jessie asked, two hours later.

He thought about her question for a moment, his fingers laced in hers across the restaurant table. He'd brought the subject of his parents up on his own, without prompting, just as they'd finished their main course, and Jessie had to fight not to read too much into such a personal topic. He needed someone to listen, that was all, and she was the person he happened to be with.

They shouldn't be touching like this, caressing each other's hands, yet she couldn't bring herself to ease hers away. All they'd done since they'd arrived at this beautiful waterfront restaurant had been talk and touch. As for eating and drinking, she'd hardly noticed any of that! But all of it felt impossibly intense, as if the talking was laying a foundation for the body magic that they could hardly wait for, and much more.

'Protective, I think,' he answered her finally. His finger stilled in hers. 'Towards both of them. Mum, in particular. If Dad hurt her again…'

'Is that what's holding her back, do you think? The risk of getting hurt?' Jessie couldn't help leaning towards him, couldn't take her eyes from his face.

'I don't know. I imagine it's more complicated than that. Their history together is so complicated after all.' He looked down, putting his eyes into shadow and making the thick crescents of his lashes look darker. 'She's a very sensible woman, my mother, but she has the capacity for strong feelings as well, and that's a difficult combination sometimes. She'll look very carefully before she leaps, because she has such a keen eye for the consequences, and such good memory for all the good and bad there was in their marriage. It's a hard ask, on his part.'

'Do you think he's aware of that?' Jessie sipped some wine absently.

Keelan looked up, and she watched his mouth—the way it pouted for a moment into a kiss shape on certain words, the way his tongue rested for a moment against his lower lip. 'Not fully. Not yet. But Mum will make damned sure that he is before she makes him any promises.'

'You sound as if you're still on her side.' She squeezed his hand, and ran the ball of her thumb lightly across his knuckles.

Again, he thought for a good while before he answered. 'I've tried not to make that too apparent to Dad, since his divorce from Louise, because that was such an admission on his part that he'd made a huge mistake. Actually, I'm just trying to be fair, and to look at the whole thing with my eyes open.'

The way he'd said his mother would. Jessie suspected they were alike in many ways, although superficially he resembled his father more. Talking with Keelan about his family on this level held a dangerous satisfaction for her. It created the illusion that she belonged.

She recognised the feeling. She'd had it before.

Last time she hadn't even tried to fight it. This time she kept up the struggle, even though she knew she'd already lost. And suddenly she found herself spilling everything to him about John, in the context of questions she and Keelan both had about marital infidelity and forgiveness, comparing what had happened between Keelan's parents with what *hadn't* happened between Audrey and John.

'And, of course, I played Louise's part.' Her hand rested on the table now, a willing prisoner beneath his.

'Not really,' he said. 'I don't think that's true, from what you've just told me.'

'The other woman? The woman who was prepared to betray someone I respected and cared about for the sake of what I thought was love?'

'Louise never respected or cared about Mum. She was terrified of her. But that's irrelevant. What I'm interested in is the fact that you still blame yourself to such an extent.'

'Shouldn't I? I was terribly in the wrong.'

'At first, I guess, but—' He switched tack suddenly. 'Did you see it coming?'

'See…?'

'What you felt. And his response.'

'No, I didn't.' She stared down at her empty plate, hardly noticing when the waiter took it away, while she was speaking. 'It blind-sided me completely. I was still calling it empathy and admiration, when suddenly he and I were alone in the kitchen one day and he took me in his arms and I discovered just how much I'd been kidding myself.'

'You might have managed to put up some barriers if you'd had more warning,' Keelan suggested.

'Maybe.'

'And you were the one who ended it.'

'For the wrong reasons.'

'No. The right ones.' He stroked a strand of uncooperative hair back from her face. 'Without Audrey herself ever knowing, and that was right, because in her situation knowing wouldn't have helped. I might concede that your wake-up call came from the wrong direction—that other woman—but when it did come, you got everything into perspective very quickly, from the sound of it.'

'Why are you working so hard to let me off the hook, Keelan?' She frowned and shook her head, unsettled by the intent way he still watched her. 'Telling you all this was supposed to be about giving you some insights into what's happening with your parents.'

'Yes?' He tilted his face, sceptical and almost teasing.

She flushed. 'Yes, I—I think so.'

'Nope.' He sounded very decisive now. 'We're not doing that at all. We're doing something else. Clearing our emotional in-trays, I think. So that there's plenty of room.'

'Room?'

'For so much else, Jessie. For holding each other, skin to skin, without any baggage getting in the way. It's my turn now—to tell you about my divorce.'

'Keelan, I don't want to weasel out anything from you that—'

'Shh… Let's just talk.' He took her hand again, and leaned across the table. 'Let's do this. Let me tell you about Tanya, and what broke us apart. I've only glossed over it to you before.'

Deep down, she wanted to hear everything and anything he wanted to tell her, so she didn't argue. He wasn't long-winded about it. A couple of years into their marriage, an old crush of Tanya's had come back into her life. Not someone she'd ever been involved with, but someone she'd wanted.

'And they had an affair?' Jessie said, when Keelan paused.

'No, they didn't. But she must have been getting signals from him. It would have been against her principles to leap into bed with him while she was still married to me, but it wasn't against her principles to sabotage our marriage in every other way she could think of. I was…totally bewildered for a long time, didn't understand that she was deliberately driving me away to leave her own slate clean.'

'Driving you away?'

What woman in her right mind could possibly do that?

Me, came an insidious little voice inside her.

Isn't that what I'm trying to do, a part of me, because I'm so sceptical and scared?

'Suddenly, everything I did was wrong,' Keelan said. 'Ranging from petty things like not buying her flowers often enough to major issues like "you don't communicate, you close yourself off," which I couldn't see the…' He stopped, then continued, 'Maybe it's a guy thing. These vague accusations, the suggestion that I was clueless because I couldn't even get a bead on the accusations, let alone address them.'

He shook his head and went on. 'I really thought, for months, that they were genuine grievances I should work on, or we should work on together. But when I tried, she upped the ante. 'Now you're just bringing me flowers because I complained. Don't you get it?' Well, no. I didn't. But it worked in the end. When we split, I thought it was a mutual decision. Amicable separation. Irreconcilable differences. You know the drill. I really thought we'd both tried. Until she flew back to New Zealand to move in with Rick just a few weeks later. He owns a big construction company there. Doing very well. They have two little girls, and I wish them well. At the time, I felt…' He shrugged.

'Conned,' Jessie suggested, because she knew about feeling conned.

Something they had in common that she would never have suspected without all the talking they'd done tonight.

'Most definitely conned,' he answered. 'Wondering why I hadn't seen what was happening while I was in the middle of it.'

'Because people don't. So often, people don't. It takes hindsight. Don't blame yourself for that, Keelan.'

'And I'm going to tell you the same thing. Don't keep racking yourself over Audrey and John. Don't see all that as a pattern you're bound to repeat.'

He said their names as if they were people he knew, and Jessie understood what a lot of ground they'd covered tonight. It felt good, but deeply dangerous as usual.

'Our waiter is hovering,' he said a moment or two later. 'Do you want dessert?'

'Real dessert?' she blurted out at once, remembering what he'd said on the beach about chocolate-dipped strawberries and whipped cream. 'Or…?'

He sat back and laughed, then leaned close again and said in a low voice, 'Believe it or not, yes, I was actually talking about real dessert. But if you're too impatient for the other kind…'

She blushed at once. 'No! I mean…' She trailed off, then took her courage in her hands, fixed her eyes on him steadily and said, 'I'm up for both.'

The house was very quiet when they got back at almost eleven. The sky had clouded over, the air had cooled and freshened, and there was no moon. Jessie thought she could smell rain in the air. She hoped everyone would sleep well tonight…

Inside, the bedrooms were dark, with doors ajar. Tavie 'pigletted' in her sleep, the sound coming through louder on the monitor in Susan's room than it did from the baby herself. In the big, open-plan living room, they discovered Dawson asleep on the couch, which had been made up with sheets, a quilt and pillows.

Their arrival had woken him, unfortunately. He stirred, sat up and said croakily, 'Back safe? That's good. She had a fussy period, but Susie got her settled.'

'Sorry to wake you, Dad.' Understatement on Keelan's part. His tone sounded a little strained.

'I should have gone for the alcove outside the laundry, but I thought your mother might need help with the baby if she woke up again before you got back, and I might not hear down there. Changed her nappy tonight,' he added, trying but failing to sound offhand about the feat. 'She kicks beautifully, doesn't she?'

'Dawson, you're not giving them a blow-by-blow description, I hope!' Lynette said, appearing in a robe from the bedroom she and Alan were using. 'Keelan and Jessie are supposed to be…' She stopped. 'Well, getting a break.'

'Hardly preventing that with a bit of a report, am I?'

But he was, of course.

Jessie felt as self-conscious as if they'd both been caught naked. Her whole body, which had been swimming with anticipation and nerves and aching, terrifying need, now felt bathed in floodlights. She hugged her arms around herself as if touching Keelan was the furthest thing from her mind.

'You're fine, Dad,' Keelan assured him, his throat rasping. 'No problem. Goodnight, now.'

Along the corridor, a minute later, he muttered darkly to Jessie, 'Are you getting a sense of *déjà vu* here?'

He brushed his knuckles from her ear to her neck to her collar-bone, painting her with a hot trail of awareness and desire. Leaving the restaurant half an hour ago, they'd paused for a long time beside the car to kiss. Here in the driveway, they'd reached for each other at once, every touch containing impatience and promise.

'I will get a very strong sense of *déjà vu* if you tell me "Later", like you did this morning,' she admitted. 'And you're going to, aren't you?'

'Is there a choice? The layout of this house does not facilitate privacy.' He pinned her against her bedroom door and traced the contours of her lips with the tip of one finger, his imposing body almost menacing her with the strength of his desire, and hers. 'Pity they didn't put one of us in the end room. I wasn't planning for this to have to be quiet and stealthy. Not at all. I want it to be anything but.' He brushed his mouth against her ear and whispered, 'Have to tell you, Jessie, I've been wondering all day if I could get you to make a lot of noise…'

'Keelan…' she breathed, throbbing deep inside.

'Thought Dad would be downstairs, and the others asleep with their doors closed.'

'There's tomorrow,' she said. 'When we get home.'

It seemed too far away, both physically and emotionally.

'There'd better be tomorrow,' he answered.

'Or there's the beach.'

Her words were punctuated by the sound of rain beginning to spatter onto the roof, and all they could do was sigh and shrug and laugh.

CHAPTER NINE

KEELAN and Jessie pulled into the hospital parking area at five the following afternoon, after an easier journey than Friday's northbound one had been and a relatively relaxing morning. They'd talked a lot, looked at each other a lot and said an impossible amount to each other with their eyes.

'She didn't wake up,' Keelan said.

'She's starting to.'

'Her first visit to her brother. Maybe she's getting excited about it.'

'The nurses will love seeing her. I want to see them deeply impressed at how much she's grown and how strong she looks.'

Impressing the nurses wouldn't be hard when they had Tam for comparison.

Back in the familiar environment of the hospital, the reality of Tam's impending surgery came crashing down on both of them again, and the fact that they didn't talk about it was more significant than if they had. Jessie knew that Keelan's thoughts would be running along the same tired, difficult track as hers.

They'd had their weekend away, and Susan and her sister, and even Keelan's father, had been unflagging in their efforts to make it easy and pleasant for the two of them and for Tavie, but this was the world they really inhabited. Jessie felt the first tinge of inner questioning about the depth and meaning of what had flared so powerfully between herself and Keelan.

Would it hold up *at all* here in the city?

Or would it all vanish, no more than a brief illusion?

Keelan had phoned the NICU late yesterday afternoon and again this morning, to receive cautiously positive reports about his little boy. Tam was hanging in there. His surgeons were confident that the planned procedure would take place. They didn't talk about the percentage chance of success, and Keelan told Jessie that he hadn't asked.

Percentages weren't relevant when there was no choice.

Nurse Barb McDaniel, who'd been one of Tavie's main carers during her stay, was rostered to look after Tam on this shift, and she was delighted to see Tam's sister again, after the two adults had been through the necessary hand-washing routine in the big sinks just beyond the unit's swing doors.

'Oh, she's amazing!' Barb said. 'Well, they always are, but this one! No, I'd love to hold her, but I won't. Keep her in her car capsule. What does she weigh now? And she's not on any oxygen or supplemental feeds any more? That's fantastic! See what your sister's given you to live up to, little man? All we need is that heart ticking over nicely, and you'll be powering along, threatening to catch up and overtake her.'

Tavie delivered a fabulous smile. She'd get hungry soon. Jessie wondered how long Keelan would want to stay. She could prepare the baby's bottle down in the car, if necessary, feed her and wait for Keelan there.

'Has he had a good weekend?' Keelan asked, standing beside the transparent humidicrib.

'Hanging in there.'

Jessie felt Keelan stiffen, wanted to run her hand down his arm in a gesture of support, but didn't dare. He swore.

'You don't know how I hate that expression now! I'm sorry, I'm not blaming you for using it, Barb. I just wish we could hear something different for a change. His colour's not very good today, is it?'

'No, he's fighting to keep those lips looking pink, and his hands are a bit too mottled for my liking. He's put on a few grams.'

'Which he could shed just as easily.'

'Did you sign the consent forms on Friday, Dr Hunter?'

'Yes, all of that.'

'And Dr Bedford outlined how he's planning to proceed?'

'In more detail than I wanted, to be honest.' Like any doctor, he knew too much, and he'd seen failure as well as miracles.

As was often done with preemies, the surgeons would perform the surgery here in the unit, tucked away in a tiny annexe room, rather than tiring Tam with a long trip down to the basement-level operating suites. It would be a lengthy process—several hours—and the apparent size and position of the largest hole, as well as its complex arrangement of entry and exit points, would dictate open heart surgery through the side of the organ.

Jessie could only imagine, but she could imagine far too vividly. She'd been in NICU units during surgery on a baby and, even though she hadn't been directly involved, she knew what it would be like.

There would be two surgeons, two nurses and an anaesthetist, all jostling for space around the tiny child. He would need minuscule doses of the required drugs—a sedative to put him to sleep, an agent to numb the surgical site itself and a narcotic for pain. As with any surgery, he'd be draped, taped and painted with a sterilising solution, and the planned line of the incision would be marked. It would no doubt look like a huge swathe of territory on his tiny torso.

When his skin had been pulled back, and the armature of muscles that stretched over his tiny ribs had been cut and folded, he would be at the mercy of surgical instruments hardly bigger than sewing pins, in the hands of a grown man's fingers that could, despite their size, move with the delicacy of a bee dancing.

The blood vessels in a baby this young and this small were not much stronger than sodden paper. Even a tiny tear in one of the really important ones could be fatal—a death dive via sudden, irreparable blood loss. The holes would be patched with a special synthetic fabric, as would the thinned section of Tam's tiny aorta. Dr Bedford would be soaked in sweat by the time he finished, even if everything went perfectly to plan.

Jessie knew how long those hours would seem for both herself and Keelan tomorrow. She'd be at home with Tavie. Keelan had commitments with his own patients. Knowing that there was nothing he could do for Tam, he hadn't tried to postpone those. They'd provide a more productive focus for his thoughts. Doubtless he would be called down to the A & E department more than once as well to give his verdict on a potential admission.

'Going to be a long day,' Barb McDaniel said, summarising, in just six short words, the track Jessie's thoughts had taken.

'Keith is starting at eight, he told me,' Keelan said. 'I'll be in here during my lunch-break—if I get one. He's hoping the surgery will be done by then.'

Tavie started to fuss a little.

'I'll take her down to the car,' Jessie said. 'Stay as long as you want, Keelan. She'll take her feed on my lap in the passenger seat. It's in the shade, nice and peaceful. Take an hour, if you want.'

'I'd like to spend some time with him,' Keelan said. 'But I'd like you to as well.'

'We'll fit that in this evening, if we can. If Tavie co-operates.'

He nodded, reached out, squeezed her hand, and like so many times before, it felt as if they were parents, sharing all of this completely, only the sensation was so much stronger today, so much more physical, buried deep inside Jessie and radiating out to her fingertips and to the sun-bleached ends of her hair.

She wanted to kiss Keelan, hold him, tell him, It's going to be all right. And she wanted to cry with him, bury her face in his shoulder and feel their bodies shaking together with inextricably mingled emotion.

Instead, all she could say in a husky voice was, 'See you in a while. Just when you're ready. Don't hurry.'

Down in the car, she cuddled little Tavie and sang to her, gave her the bottle she'd prepared earlier—which Tavie was generous enough to take colder than usual—and even played peek-a-boo.

'This is probably a little too advanced for you, sweetheart, but it's keeping *me* entertained, and I need that right now!'

Tavie was fast asleep again by the time Keelan appeared. He looked very strained, and didn't say much in the car. Jessie didn't need to ask why. Tavie had one of her fussy periods in the evening, which turned a simple dinner of ham and cheese omelettes into a lengthy process during which the two adults never got to sit down at the same time.

'Let me take care of her now,' Jessie said at eight o'clock.

'No, I really want you to go back up to the hospital.'

And she knew that in the back of Keelan's mind, although he'd never say it out loud, was the fear that if she didn't go and see Tam tonight, she'd miss out on her last chance to say goodbye.

Keelan was shameless in his need to anaesthetise himself after Jessie had gone to the hospital. He got Tavie ready for bed and tried rocking her in the chair in her room, but she remained fussy so he gave up and went back downstairs, found himself a beer and the junkiest television on offer.

Maybe the baby had been sensing his tension. Now that he sat sprawled on the couch, absorbed in the nth repeat of a paint-by-numbers, G-rated action movie, Tavie seemed ready to sleep more peacefully. She lay in a warm little bundle with her body on his chest and her head on his shoulder, and he could feel the tiny puffs of her warm, milky breath on his neck. The pictures on the television screen provided the only light, and her little face lay in shadow.

He didn't want to have another try at putting her in her cot. Just didn't want to move. So they both stayed put.

What a weekend!

Two major undercurrents of unresolved feeling still twisted together inside him even now. Tam was having life-or-death surgery tomorrow, and he and Jessie were desperate to sleep together, with the entire universe apparently conspiring to prevent it.

He'd learned a lot more about her over the weekend—her doubts, her vulnerabilities and her strengths. He knew, now, how much of that footloose attitude of hers was just a protection. And he also knew that she was nothing like his father's second wife.

Which left him with very few barriers in place in his feelings about Tam and his feelings about Jessica Russell.

Pretty tough to live through.

He still wondered about his parents, too, and whether they'd really have a second attempt at their marriage. It looked distinctly possible, after what he'd seen yesterday and today.

Meanwhile, by one definition, he and Jessie were already up to the third attempt at theirs.

Tonight? When she got back from the hospital?

No. Hardly seemed possible that she'd want to. He wasn't crass enough to toss Tavie into her cot like a football so that he had his hands free for ripping off the nurse's clothes.

He ached.

Focus on the movie, Hunter. Pretend you don't already know exactly what's going to happen in every scene.

His eyelids began to feel heavy and his limbs relaxed. Tavie had the right idea. Jessie would be back soon. She'd wake him up if necessary. Sleep was a refuge that had eluded him for most of last night, and he knew he'd wake early in the morning. If he could flick off the television with the remote control and snatch some now…

The first he knew of Jessie's return was the feel of her hands as she gently lifted the sleeping baby from his chest. He dragged his eyes open, but she told him in a whisper, 'Don't move. I'll take her upstairs. Just stay right there.'

Tavie stirred a little but remained asleep, and Jessie wasn't gone long. When she returned, Keelan was still groggily attempting to wake up enough to move. Within two seconds he was as awake as he'd ever been in his life, and one part of him, at least, was moving just as nature intended.

Jessie's lush, firm rear end had planted itself squarely and confidently on his thighs, and two soft arms had wound around his neck. 'I'm sorry I was at the hospital so long. It was—Tam was…hard to leave. But I'm…'

She stopped, must have sensed the initial tensing of his muscles in sheer surprise. Her voice faltered. 'Keelan? Isn't this…?'

'Yes.' He swore. 'Yes! It's what I wanted, and want. Painfully. But after a long day—after *this* day—I thought that you might have changed your mind, lost your—'

'No,' she said, without hesitation. 'No.'

Keelan's whole body surged, charged with electricity, burst into flames. He stole the initiative from her openly at once, slipping one hand between her thighs and curving the other around her neck to pull her against his mouth. Her lips were warm and sweet and hungry.

He kissed her until they were both breathless and dizzy and half-drunk with the taste of each other, and he kept on kissing her because it felt so fabulous to get utterly lost in her like this.

Eventually, with eyes closed and fingers gripping his shoulders for support, she pivoted to straddle him. He loved her impatience, and the way it was so obvious how much more she wanted, how much closer she wanted their contact to be. Her knees pressed into the back of the couch, and her breasts felt heavy and powerfully erotic against his chest. He cupped his hands around her hips and wondered how they'd get upstairs, then just a few seconds later, *if* they'd get upstairs.

When she eased herself back from his touch, crossed her arms across her front and pulled off that same thin, figure-hugging blue sweater she'd worn yesterday morning and got herself tangled in against the corridor wall of his mother's house, Keelan abandoned any more thought of moving anywhere.

This was going to happen right here and now. Only…

'We have no protection,' he managed to say.

'Yes, we do…' She pulled something from her pocket, pressed it into his hand, then blushed and looked touchingly uncertain. 'I thought of it. Is that…?'

Shameful? Was that the word she couldn't quite say?

'It's enough reason for my lifelong gratitude, Jessie,' he told her seriously.

Her breasts were fabulous, and swollen dramatically with passion, their nipples hard through her skin-toned bra. Deftly, she unclipped it and he pulled it down, loving the way the cups fell from her body to release her weight into his hands.

She closed her eyes again, hair spilling over her face like a drift of autumn leaves caught by a breeze. Her body shuddered at every touch he made, and her breath went in an out like that of an athlete after a race.

Her responsiveness made the electric charge in his own body even stronger.

Somehow they moved until they lay horizontal on the long couch, again with Jessie poised over him, hair hiding her face, rock-hard, darkened nipples pushing on him, sending their message of pleasure and need.

'How much patience do you have?' he growled at her.

'None.' The word hardly counted as speech, it had so much breath in it.

'Good.'

He snapped open the fastening on her jeans and began to drag them down. She helped him, shimmying her hips in a way that had his own dark trousers stretched painfully tight across the front. Her body could rock like a belly dancer, and he wanted to rock with her. After a little clumsiness, a little laughter and a lot of distracted, desperate caresses, they had nothing getting in the way any more, except that small piece of latex she'd been so unsure about, and he strained against the soft heat of her lower stomach which pressed on top of him, making him crazy every time he let himself slip.

'You're so perfect,' he told her. 'Your skin, your shape, the way you move.'

'So are you. Don't wait. Let me feel you.'

They rolled and she held up her arms, shaped herself for him and made his entry effortless. He shuddered and she held him, her breath coming in time to his own rhythm, her warmth enfolding him in an ecstasy that clawed higher and higher. It seemed impossible that the peak they surged towards could be any steeper, any further, yet the climb continued and every second of it felt better than the last.

He felt the exact moment when her world spun out of control, felt the dig of her nails in his back, moved in unison with the whip of her hips and spine, and heard the cries from her that vibrated like the soundbox of a cello. Then his own cries overtook hers, the last remnant of his control shattered into a million pieces, and his senses blurred and merged into one dark, headlong current.

They lay tangled together afterwards for a long time, too overwhelmed to speak. And, anyway, hadn't their bodies already said everything about how perfect and earth-shattering their love-making had been?

Keelan kissed Jessie's hair, her temple, her shoulder, deeply savouring his right of possession, the way he could hold her and touch her wherever he wanted, without any fear of protest or of overstepping her boundaries.

There was something so generous about her. Courageous, too. To have given herself like this, to the babies and to him, without the promise of anything in return. Keelan knew he'd short-changed her in suggesting a cool-headed affair. Tavie was at least giving smiles in payment now, but Tam hadn't yet even promised to live.

A sour jet of fear surged inside him as he thought this, giving his mouth an unpleasant taste, and he shut his eyes blindly to any consideration of the future. He could make no promises right now. Not to Jessie, and not to himself. Maybe everything they both felt had far more to do with Tam than either of them had realised.

In all honesty, he couldn't discount this possibility, because he knew it happened to people all the time. In war, in grief, in crisis. When your gut was churning with fear about the future, about the prospect of gut-wrenching loss, you didn't know what you would feel about each other this time next year, or next month, or even next week.

Kissing her one last time, in the soft curve of her neck, he murmured, 'It's late, Jessie.'

Her eyes looked soft and sleepy and full of questions. She wanted more.

Women usually did, and in the past he'd always been happy to give it, and say it. 'I'll phone you tomorrow evening,' or 'That was amazing,' or 'Can't wait till I can see you again.' After he and Tanya had slept together for the first time, he'd said, 'I love you,' without hesitation.

Tonight, however, he couldn't think of anything that would be safe or fair. He knew he didn't want to hurt Jessie. Or himself.

In the end, all he said was, 'Sleep well,' hearing the inadequacy of the line but knowing he had nothing better.

She nodded and gave a tentative smile. 'You, too.'

Then she disappeared up the stairs on soft feet, her bundled clothing gathered in her arms and her bare, pale body vulnerable in a way it hadn't been as they'd made love.

Keelan listened in the darkness and heard the movements she made as she prepared for bed. Water ran through the pipes, and a couple of floorboards creaked. A faint light came from her room and reflected against the wall that flanked the stairs, but then it ebbed away as she closed her bedroom door.

He waited another few seconds until no more sounds filtered down, and only then did he make a move himself.

Jessie had known that the following morning would be endless, and it was.

The night hadn't exactly passed in the blink of an eye either. Having dozed and dreamed for long, delicious minutes in Keelan's arms on the couch, she had lain awake as restless and jittery as a caffeine addict once she'd reached her own bed.

She'd wanted Keelan beside her so badly, but he hadn't come.

Why?

Regret, already, about what they'd just done?

Or was it only women who felt that kind of remorse? Maybe he'd simply felt a replete and very male sense of release which had launched him into an excellent night's sleep.

Oh, and he probably needed it!

She couldn't be selfish enough to wish her own restlessness on him when he must be so worried, as she was, about Tam. And she couldn't expect that the way they'd made love had tilted his whole universe, the way it had tilted hers.

At six in the morning, Tavie announced loudly that she was awake and hungry and ready to play. Jessie went to her and tried to gain a sense of peace and contentment from the feel of that warm, delicious little body, and the huge smile that came in the middle of Tavie's feed so that milk pooled in the baby's pink mouth and ran out at the corners.

'Angel sweetheart,' she whispered to the little girl. 'Precious darling. Gosh, I love you!'

Tavie thought that was fine.

Tavie didn't know what her brother had to go through today.

Jessie still had the baby on her lap when she heard Keelan in his room, and then the faint, rhythmic thrum of water piping into his shower. He appeared a few minutes later. 'I'm heading straight to the hospital,' he said. 'I'll grab breakfast there later.'

'And you'll phone me as soon as—'

'Of course. I can't promise when you'll get to see him, though.'

'That's all right.'

'You should be there. This is so…' He stopped, opened his hands. 'Backwards somehow. Wrong.' He scraped his fingers across his newly shaven jaw, and they almost looked as if they were shaking. 'But I don't know what to do about that.'

'It's OK.' She had to tell him so, because the last thing he needed was a litany of all the reasons why it wasn't OK at all.

'I'll be home when I can. If Mica is free this afternoon, get her to stay on. Leave Tavie with her and come up. See you some time.'

'Yes. See you.' She couldn't manage more than this, and he didn't wait.

She heard him leave the house just a few minutes later.

Mrs Sagovic arrived at eight-thirty. She hadn't been here on Friday, so she didn't yet know that Tam was scheduled for surgery today. When Jessie told her, she threw up her hands then clasped them together, her eyes bright with tears. 'That tiny boy!' She'd seen how fragile he was in the photos that Keelan and Jessie had both taken. 'I can't believe it!'

'There was no choice, Mica. It's the last throw of the dice.'

'And you're not there?'

Jessie shrugged. 'I'm here. With Tavie. I couldn't have stood in on the surgery, and I wouldn't have wanted to. And what's the use of just pacing the corridors outside? If it goes badly…' She didn't even want to say it.

The housekeeper hugged her, and murmured something in her mother tongue.

'Keelan did wonder if you could stay this afternoon so I can go up there then,' Jessie said.

'And where is he?'

'With patients.'

'Of course I can stay. Whether I can push myself together to clean Dr Hunter's house is another story!' She threw up her work hardened hands again and cried, 'That little boy…'

'Keelan is going to phone when there's some news. He doesn't think it'll be before lunch.'

'Then that's when you should go to the hospital. At lunch. That man needs someone with him.'

'His mother wanted to come down, but he wouldn't let her, in case—in case the surgery went—'

'What does ''let'' mean?' Mrs Sagovic cut in. 'She should have come anyway!'

The housekeeper's manner suggested that these

Australians of northern European origin didn't have the slightest idea when it came to family relationships, compared to people who shared her own Mediterranean heritage. She probably wouldn't have been impressed with Jessie's parents, or with Brooke Hunter's mother, Louise.

But she'd underestimated Keelan's mother, as it turned out.

Susan arrived at just before noon. 'I couldn't wait for a phone call.' She hugged Jessie, seeming warm and a little shaky—tired, too, after the drive.

Dawson had driven back to Sydney yesterday afternoon, and Jessie took a moment to wonder whether the two of them would see each other while Susan was down.

'I can't wait for a phone call either,' Jessie answered frankly. 'But no one's taking any notice of that. He hasn't phoned.'

'Which can only mean the baby's still in surgery. Can't believe it can take that long and still have any chance of success.'

'Can I drive you up, Susan? Mica's ready to push me out of the house. She'll think we're incurably wrong-headed if we don't go.'

'Yes, can you drive me? Please? We *are* incurably wrong-headed if we don't go, but I'm not sure that I could get back behind the wheel. I would have gone straight there, only…I'm terrified. I'm so scared.'

'Mmm.' Jessie nodded, her throat tight.

'Let me bring in my bags…'

Jessie helped, and then the two of them took Keelan's second car, ushered there by approving nods and pats from Mrs Sagovic. 'Yes, I know the baby is waking up. I can take care of her. You must go.'

* * *

The unit seemed quiet when they arrived, and the door to the annexe was still firmly closed. 'The team's still in there?' Jessie asked Stephanie.

'Yes, they are.'

'I thought surely…'

The other nurse shrugged and smiled, then said, 'Dr Hunter was called down from Paediatrics about ten minutes ago. He'll be here soon.'

'So we wait,' Susan murmured.

'We wait,' Jessie confirmed.

The wait wasn't long. Only about six hundred heartbeats, every one of which Jessie felt like a painful blow in her chest. Keelan arrived, and didn't seem all that surprised to see his mother. He managed a pale smile and a few token words of greeting, and he hardly seemed to look at Jessie at all.

Which in the greater scheme of things didn't matter right now, but…

Then suddenly Keith Bedford appeared, surgical mask still in his hand and clothing darkened with moisture. He put his hand on Keelan's arm. 'We had some problems, I'm afraid,' he said.

CHAPTER TEN

'WHAT problems?' Keelan's white lips hardly moved.

Having beat so painfully for ten minutes, Jessie's heart now didn't seem to be beating at all, and that was worse. She couldn't speak, but heard the stricken sound that came from Susan's throat, beside her.

'Well, the surgery itself went better than expected in many ways,' Dr Bedford said. 'One of the holes was small enough to leave alone. It'll close over on its own. The biggest, yes, was very tricky but we made a successful repair, as we did with the other two moderate-size holes and the thinned section of aorta. Unfortunately, right in the middle of it all, Tam developed a third-degree AV block.'

Susan cast a terrified, questioning look at Jessie, but she could only shake her head. She knew what Dr Bedford was talking about. The electrical impulses in the baby's heart had been slowed or blocked somehow, and had ceased to take their normal path through the heart's conduction system, resulting in compromised or, in the most extreme scenario, non-existent electrical communication between the heart's upper and lower chambers—the atria and the ventricles.

Sometimes the lower heart chambers generated electrical impulses on their own, but these weren't enough to keep the heart muscle at full function. There was a serious risk of full cardiac arrest. Had this happened to Tam?

But she couldn't explain something so complex and

technical to Susan now, not while the heart surgeon was still speaking, not while she didn't yet know what the outcome had been.

'We've put in an external pacemaker wire,' the surgeon said.

'And he's survived? He's...' Keelan slowed and shaped his mouth carefully around the phrase Jessie knew he hated. 'Hanging in there?'

'Yes. He's doing well. But you know the consequences of this, Keelan. If his heart doesn't resume its natural pacing on its own, he'll need further surgery to implant a permanent pacemaker.'

'OK.' Keelan gave a brief, jerky nod. 'How long will you give him before a decision on that is made?'

'If it hasn't happened within a few days, then it's not going to. After that has become evident, if it becomes evident, we'll wait until he's recovered from today's surgery and then go in again. Obviously, it's a much more minor procedure.'

Jessie heard Susan give a cautious, shaky sigh of relief at this final piece of comparative good news.

'Can we see him?' Keelan asked.

Dr Bedford narrowed his eyes. 'Not all three of you. Not yet. Two of you. And I want you in masks, caps, gowns and shoe covers. I'm keeping him in the annexe until someone else needs the space, basically. At least twenty-four hours, I hope, and preferably longer. This has been touch and go for him the whole way. And it still is.'

'Two of us,' Keelan muttered.

'For a couple of minutes. Bevan's still monitoring the reversal of the anaesthesia. Page me if you have any questions. I'll be in again to look at him later this afternoon. But you know what to look for yourself, what to expect.'

Keelan only nodded. His eyes flicked to Jessie, and then to his mother.

'You see him, Susan,' Jessie said quickly. Her throat felt as if there was a bone lodged in it, sideways.

'No, Jessie. I want you to go.'

Jessie closed her eyes. Susan was being incredibly generous, but a grandmother took precedence over an employee, and officially that was all she was. 'No,' she said. She had to fight so hard to keep her voice firm that it sounded almost angry. 'I'm not. You must. With Keelan.'

This time nobody argued.

Nervously, Susan accepted Keelan's guidance in putting on the sterile garments Dr Bedford had required. The bright royal blue of the stiff disposable fabric cap seemed to suck the colour away from her face. She wasn't a large or imposing woman, but Jessie hadn't really registered her slightness of build until now. Normally she carried with her such a strong sense of life, but at this moment she looked shrunken in trepidation.

And, of course, she was the right person to go.

Keelan touched the heel of his hand lightly to his mother's back, propelling her in the direction of the annexe where Tam still lay, and within a half minute they had disappeared, leaving Jessie alone.

She felt empty, frozen, grief-stricken. Keith Bedford's casual decree that Tam couldn't yet be crowded with more than two visitors had only emphasised the uncertainty that coloured everything she felt.

It surely wouldn't have eased her fears over Tam if she had known exactly where she fitted into Keelan's life—his present and his future. And yet, perversely, she felt that nothing could be harder than the way she felt now.

She was so scared for Tam, and yet she didn't remotely know if she had the right to take comfort in the love for Tavie that grew stronger inside her every day, let alone the love for Keelan that felt like something she'd known since she'd entered this world, and would know, just as painfully as this, until she left it again.

All of that might end in a matter of weeks, when Keelan decided he didn't need her any more.

Keelan and Susan weren't with the baby for long. He had his hand on her shoulder when they came out, and Jessie could see that Susan had found it very emotional, and very hard, to see the way her little grandson must look—motionless enough to seem frozen, lost in wires, his chest seemingly weighed down and lopsided with a dressing that would be huge and terrifying on such a tiny body.

'The monitors say he's alive. That was the only way I knew,' Susan said.

'His colour looked good,' Keelan said. 'He looked good.'

Jessie nodded. Colour was important. You clung to things like a baby's colour at a time like this.

'Can I take these things off now, love?' Susan asked.

'Yes, Mum, that's fine. There's a bin just outside.' He pressed his fingertips to the bridge of his nose. 'Then, do you need me to…? What do you need me to do?'

'Tell me where the cafeteria is, because I need some tea.'

'Something to eat, too. You look pale.'

'A sandwich. Just show me where it is.' She hung on his arm, apparently in need of the support.

Not knowing what was expected of her, Jessie went

down with them in the lift. She let them get out first, then peeled off quietly in the direction of a visitors' bathroom. She didn't think they'd noticed.

Later, she would find Susan in the cafeteria, because the older woman would probably want to be taken home. Meanwhile, not the slightest bit hungry, Jessie decided she would go outside for a bit and find some fresh air and some sun for her face, out by the little piece of garden that flanked the hospital's original colonial-era building.

It must have been ten or fifteen minutes before Keelan found her, and one look at him striding across the grass towards her told her how angry he was. Tight lines etched his face, and his shoulders had tensed and lifted as if padded like an American football player's.

'Where the hell did you get to?' he demanded. 'I looked around and you'd disappeared. Not a word. When? Why?'

'I wasn't hungry.'

He swore. 'Is that an answer?' His hands closed hard around her upper arms. 'You came down with us in the lift, and then you disappeared.'

In a shaky voice, she tried to make light of it. 'I'm here now, aren't I? Didn't vanish forever.'

'Made me realise, once and for all, how I'd feel if you did,' he growled, so low that she wasn't convinced she'd heard him right.

'How you'd feel if I…?'

'Vanished forever.'

'Abducted by space aliens?'

'Stop!' He bent and pressed his forehead against hers. 'Jessie, last night…last night…'

'Was pretty good, I thought,' she murmured.

He had his arms around her now, chafing her softly,

squeezing her as if he couldn't hold her tightly enough and never wanted to let her go. It was the best feeling she'd had all day, and it gave her just a little bit of courage—enough to let him know just a little bit about how she felt. She looked up into his face, and saw the light and the determination there.

'It was more than good,' he said. 'It was amazing. Fabulous. Unique. Perfect. And I didn't say that.'

'No, you didn't.'

'Because I didn't want to send the wrong message. What might be the wrong message,' he corrected himself quickly. 'I couldn't think straight, didn't trust anything about how I felt—last night, the whole weekend, weeks ago. And I'm still not sure if—'

'I understand, Keelan,' she cut in. 'I understand how impossible it is for you to be sure about anything right now.'

'No.' He pressed a finger to her lips. 'Now I'm sure about quite a few things. I'm not sure, though, if I was right to hold back last night. How much did that hurt, Jessie? How much did that leave you in the lurch?'

'Well, it did,' she admitted. 'Both those things.'

'Will it undo the hurt if I don't leave you in the lurch any longer?' He didn't wait for her to answer. 'I love you. That's the only way any of this fits together. I couldn't see it, couldn't feel it properly before, for so many reasons. And when I did feel it, I didn't trust it. But now… I was burning to say it as soon as we'd seen Tam, wanted to point out the cafeteria sign to Mum and tell her, "Follow that." But then I turned to check on you, and you'd just gone.'

'Only to the bathroom. You didn't notice.'

'No, I damn well didn't! But that doesn't mean— When I had to choose between you and Mum coming in to see Tam just now, and you jumped in and chose for me, and you chose Mum, it was so wrong.'

'No. Tam's grandmother...'

He ignored her. 'Totally my fault. I could see that. It stuck in my throat, too late to do anything about it then, until I could get you alone, as soon as I'd got Mum to the damned cafeteria. I hung back last night, doubting the best love-making of my life, and in doing that I denied you the right to see the baby you should be able to call yours, and I didn't want to wait a moment longer to give you that right.'

He stopped, as if suddenly unsure.

'If you want it,' he continued. 'If you want to call him yours. Do you, Jessie? Will you be my wife? Can we make a family together, so that Tam and Tavie can be yours for the rest of their lives?'

'Ours,' she whispered, holding him more tightly and pillowing her head against his chest. 'That's what I want. For them to be ours.'

'Ours. Yes. Ours.' He pressed his face into her neck and hair, and time seemed to stop in the hospital garden, even though the shadow on the old sundial crept several degrees around the tarnished bronze face.

'It's not an easy way to start,' Keelan told Jessie finally.

'I've never looked for things that were easy.'

He pulled back a little and looked at her, his face set and serious. 'No. I know. But you've made everything so much easier for me from the moment you walked off that plane nearly three months ago. Can't imagine how I'd ever do without it.'

'Neither can I. Keelan, I've come home...'

'Just where I want you. Can't believe I'm this lucky.

Can't help hoping it's part of a pattern, and that Tam's going to be this lucky, too.'

'Oh, yes.' She pressed her cheek against his, then instinctively they both turned so that their mouths met in the kiss of two people in love, sharing their hope and their fear, knowing this was only the beginning. 'He has to be this lucky. He's fought so hard.'

At almost the same time, high up in the hospital building, a little boy's heart remembered how it was supposed to beat. The pacemaker wire came out that same afternoon. After that day, Tam never looked back, never took a backward step, and neither did his parents.

Three months later, Tam and Tavie both attended a Sydney garden wedding that made everybody in the Hunter clan very happy. The bride looked radiant. The groom looked as if he'd discovered the secret to eternal youth…

And the bride and groom's thirty-five-year-old son stood with his fiancée at his side and a healthy baby girl in his arms, and had a hard time keeping his feelings in check.

'Are you taking notes?' Keelan whispered to his future bride as he watched his parents saying their vows. 'We have our own wedding coming up pretty soon, and you keep telling me I haven't got long to decide on the wording of the ceremony.'

'Thirty-five days. Not that I'm counting,' Jessie whispered back.

'I'm counting. Can't wait.'

'We haven't waited for very much, as far as I can work out,' she teased him. 'We're living under the same roof. We're already parents.'

'Can't wait for the honeymoon.'

'Oh, that. Oh, yes, that! We do have to wait a bit longer for that.'

Jessie blushed and laughed and closed her eyes to receive Keelan's kiss, while baby Tam cooed in her arms and closed his little fist against her heart.

MILLS & BOON®

Live the emotion

SEPTEMBER 2004 HARDBACK TITLES

ROMANCE™

The Mistress Wife *Lynne Graham*	H6052	0 263 18331 9
The Outback Bridal Rescue *Emma Darcy*	H6053	0 263 18332 7
The Greek's Ultimate Revenge *Julia James*	H6054	0 263 18333 5
The Frenchman's Mistress *Kathryn Ross*	H6055	0 263 18334 3
The Billionaire's Passion *Robyn Donald*	H6056	0 263 18335 1
The Moretti Marriage *Catherine Spencer*	H6057	0 263 18336 X
The Italian's Virgin Bride *Trish Morey*	H6058	0 263 18337 8
The Wealthy Man's Waitress *Maggie Cox*	H6059	0 263 18338 6
The Australian Tycoon's Proposal *Margaret Way*	H6060	0 263 18339 4
Christmas Eve Marriage *Jessica Hart*	H6061	0 263 18340 8
The Dating Resolution *Hannah Bernard*	H6062	0 263 18341 6
The Game Show Bride *Jackie Braun*	H6063	0 263 18342 4
Fill-In Fiancée *DeAnna Talcott*	H6064	0 263 18343 2
Guess Who's Coming for Christmas? *Cara Colter*	H6065	0 263 18344 0
The Police Doctor's Secret *Marion Lennox*	H6066	0 263 18345 9
Caring For His Babies *Lilian Darcy*	H6067	0 263 18346 7

HISTORICAL ROMANCE™

The Daring Duchess *Paula Marshall*	H583	0 263 18411 0
My Lady Angel *Joanna Maitland*	H584	0 263 18412 9

MEDICAL ROMANCE™

The Doctor's Christmas Bride *Sarah Morgan*	M501	0 263 18435 8
The Recovery Assignment *Alison Roberts*	M502	0 263 18436 6

0804 Gen Std HB

OCTOBER 2014 LARGE PRINT TITLES

[illegible]